Janet Lee's manuscript for *The Killing of Louisa* won the Emerging Queensland Writer category in the 2017 Queensland Literary Awards. She has a Doctor of Creative Arts from the University of the Sunshine Coast. Janet lives in south-east Queensland with her family.

The KILLING of LOUISA

JANET LEE

UQP

First published 2018 by University of Queensland Press
PO Box 6042, St Lucia, Queensland 4067 Australia

uqp.com.au
uqp@uqp.uq.edu.au

Copyright © Janet Lee 2018
The moral rights of the author have been asserted.

This book is copyright. Except for private study, research, criticism or reviews, as permitted under the *Copyright Act*, no part of this book may be reproduced, stored in a retrieval system, or transmitted in any form or by any means without prior written permission. Enquiries should be made to the publisher.

Cover design by Lisa White
Author photograph by Photography by Bambi
Typeset in 12/16 pt Bembo Std by Post Pre-press Group, Brisbane
Printed in Australia by McPherson's Printing Group, Melbourne

This novel is entirely a work of fiction. Some of the names, characters and incidents portrayed in it, while based on real historical figures, are the work of the author's imagination.

The University of Queensland Press is supported by the Queensland Government through Arts Queensland.

The University of Queensland Press is assisted by the Australian Government through the Australia Council, its arts funding and advisory body.

A catalogue record for this book is available from the National Library of Australia

ISBN 978 0 7022 6022 3 (pbk)
ISBN 978 0 7022 6160 2 (pdf)
ISBN 978 0 7022 6161 9 (epub)
ISBN 978 0 7022 6162 6 (kindle)

University of Queensland Press uses papers that are natural, renewable and recyclable products made from wood grown in sustainable forests.
The logging and manufacturing processes conform to the environmental regulations of the country of origin.

For my husband.

Legislative Assembly
19 December 1888

Mr. MELVILLE called attention to the case of Louisa Collins, sentenced to be hanged for murdering her husband. He pointed out that, after two juries had disagreed, the Crown charged her with murdering the first husband, and the jury again disagreed. He challenged the Minister of Justice to give a parallel case in the history of New South Wales. She was then tried again on the charge of murdering her second husband.

The Sydney Morning Herald[1]

Prologue

Darlinghurst Gaol, Sydney

8 January 1889

I dreamt I was walking in the tunnel, the one I walked from the gaol to my trials at the courthouse. I walked down the sandstone steps and into the darkness.

There, my warder, Alice, was waiting for me. She smiled and beckoned me to walk on. Then both my husbands walked alongside me instead.

I turned first this way and smiled at Charles and then turned and smiled at Michael.

Michael carried our baby, John. The baby wasn't crying any more, but laughing and gurgling, fat and healthy, as he never was when he was alive.

There was a light at the end of the tunnel and by that light I could see May, and she ran towards me. She wore a white dress and new black boots. In her hair was a blue ribbon embroidered with bluebirds. She took my hand and she said, I love you Ma, and I bent down and kissed her. Then my other little children all appeared and together we walked down the tunnel, into the light, and I could see a table covered with food.

They took treats from the table and ate them and laughed and danced as they did when I held the wake for Charles.

When I came up to the end of the tunnel and into the light the other children ran back the way I had just come and I could see them disappearing into the darkness.

Michael held out John in his arms and I bent to take him, but as soon as I held the baby he shrank back into the fretful child he had been in life and he began to cry and squirm. Charles reached down to the table and then turned to me with something in his hands. He smiled and held up a glass.

Drink? he said.

I handed John back to Michael, and the child was quiet.

I looked at the glass which Charles held, and I nodded; the glass was a nobbler from the hotel. Just like the one the lawyers said had sat upon the shelf in the kitchen at home, the one they said sat in the courtroom each day.

Charles reached over and took up a small jug from the table. He filled the glass with milk. I took the glass and lifted it to my lips.

Drink, Charles said again.

I drank.

I tasted the milk, but it was off and I spat it out.

They laughed at me.

They tipped their heads back and roared.

Too bitter for you, Louie? Michael asked.

Charles shook his finger at me. Drunk again, Louisa, he said. This has to stop.

Then May pointed at the table.

I saw the box, she said. I saw the rats.

I looked to where she was pointing, down at the table, and the treats were gone. The table was covered with rats, dead, lying on their backs, open boxes of Rough on Rats all around them.

I dropped the glass and clutched my throat. The rats came alive and began chasing me. I started running, running back to my prison. The light faded, and the tunnel lengthened, but I kept running.

When I wake, my heart is pounding and my skin is alive with sweat. I have a terrible pain in my guts, and hurry to the bucket which sits in my cell and serves as my privy.

As the pain eases, and my bowels finish, I will my heart to slow and I calm myself that I am well.

I tell myself that I've just had a bad dream and this has scared me into the pain I feel in my guts.

I tell myself I did not drink the milk, that there was no poison, there was none in the glass.

I tell myself there never was none.

Then I realise, though I am awake, the nightmare has not yet ended.

For today is the day I might hang.

Prisoner's Letters – Passed by Permission
From Prisoner LOUISA COLLINS
September 1888

To The Sheriff
Sir,

Permit me most respectfully to address you, I implore you to take notice to these few humble lines. My religion is Church of England. The Church of England Minister visits me on occasions. The subject is not religion I wish to speak of tis about my late husband Michael Peter Collins, was a Roman Catholic and when he took ill I wanted to send for the priest in fact I begged of him to let me send for the priest. He said no my love I will neither see priest or parson. I only want you. I dont wish to see any body I could not in any way persuade him to see the priest while he was alive. So after his death I sent for the one at Randwick as there are none living in Botany. The priest came in his buggy to my place. He had scarcely alighted when the two Botany Police that was stationary on my house all that morning I certainly thought they were friends. But later on I discovered that Doctors Marshall and Martin had ordered them to do so. When the priest was about come to my door the police detained him for a considerable time talking to him. I wondered at the delay I then sent some one to invite the priest in. He came in and read prayers over the dead body of my husband that was laying on the bed, spoke a few kind words to me and then he left. What I want to find out is this. What was the police saying to the priest. And why delay him when I sent for him.

The Sheriff
Sir,

I beg of you to grant me permission to see the two Sisters of Mercy that visits this gaol. I am sure they would only be too glad to take pitty on me and see the preist in Randwick. I am sure it would throw some light on the subject of the death of my late husband Collins which is schrouded in mystery at the present time. I asked Governor Reads permission to see the Sisters and have made several other requests of him since I have been in gaol. And he refuses me. In fact he most grossly insults me and speaks to me as though I was one void of feeling. I am only waiting trial as you know. If he is the gaoler over a few prisoners and captives he is a man ought to know better how to speak to a woman in my sad posistion.

To The Sheriff
Sir,

I cannot write myself but if you will grant permission to the authoritys to allow me, a prisoner woman, for I have some awful disclosures to make before my trials comes of which will make things look very different to what they do at the present time.

Praying that you may be pleased to grant my humble requests.

Most Humble and respectfull,

Louisa Collins[2]

1.

Darlinghurst Gaol, Sydney

26 November 1888

I am lying in the dark in my cell, straining my ears to hear the sounds of the birds waking in the pre-dawn. I think about how they fly wherever they might wish. And how I cannot fly.

Other times when I wake, I lie and think of how it is only here, in prison, that I am really free. I am not woken by a baby wanting to be put at my breast, or by a man needing me. I do not have to wash and clean and cook, although there are those in the gaol who do. But I am not a convicted woman and I have been busy attending my many trials so I am not given these jobs to do every day, though I have attended to the needlework on occasion. In my cell, there is a small window which does nothing to bring in fresh air or light and serves only to let in the flies and bugs that they might visit the slop bucket and then crawl over me.

I've been convicted of no crime, but I have been locked up all the same. They are saying I killed my husbands. They say that I killed Charles Andrews so that I might marry Michael Collins.

They say that then I killed Michael Collins. And at the inquest they tried to say I killed my own child John as well, but they could not prove that to the inquest jury.

The inquest juries said I poisoned my husbands.

And now they say in my trials as I done it with Rough on Rats.

I have been talked about at two inquests and three trials, and though the juries at the inquests said they thought I poisoned my husbands, there has been no trial jury who will say I am a murderess. So the court keeps me locked here while they search to find some other men who will think I done it. How long can they hold me here and keep looking? I think they can hold me as long as they want, and even though I have written to the Sheriff in a most respectful way, he has not helped me. The Prison Governor treats me as though I done what they say I done.

He holds me here in gaol.

There are many who speak against me, but it is my own daughter, my May, whose words hurt me the most in court. May tells them that I kept poison in the house. But what good housewife in Botany doesn't, on account of the rats coming for the blood from the sheep skins used in the tanning factories? I kept Rough on Rats, and I used it on occasion, as it was the best poison to kill. Everyone said so, including the Botany grocer, Mr Sayers.

He did not sell it at his shop, but other shops did, and in some Sydney stores you could buy Rough on Rats when you bought your devilled ham or baking powder.

They don't charge everyone who buys a box at a shop with murder.

May had talked to her little friend Florry and told her about finding the Rough on Rats box when May was in the kitchen and of how she told me so, and now everyone wonders whether

I hid the box after that. Of course I hid it. I had thought I kept the box well out of the reach of the children, but after May found it, I took the box from the high shelf and put it somewhere else, where she would not find it again.

That was my crime.

I should never have done it.

Then the police got my girl, who was only ten at the time, and the lawyers placed her in the witness box, though she could hardly see over the top of it, and then they made her words sound so she would damn her mother. She gave her testimony and whenever she stumbled over her words, they questioned her again and again and she is only a child.

She said she had seen the box in the kitchen, and that she seen it the week before Michael Collins had died. And she said that it was a little round box with a lid. What was on the box? they said, and the lawyer spoke about it for a considerable time, and put the words into her mouth, asking if there were pictures on the box, and my May, well, first she said there was nothing on the outside. So they asked her again. Was she sure? they said and I think they prompted her to think of something she should say, so she nodded. Pictures of rats, she said, and the rats were red, lying on their backs. And the lawyer asked could she name the box, and she said she could, and that she had told me at the time. She told the court she said, Look what I've found on the shelf, Ma, and that she read the label to me: Rough on Rats.

Now she just recites the story every time.

And I have to watch while the lawyers and judges say, Thank you, May, and smile at her, smug as you like.

The child would not know how her words make it look like I done it.

But they never asked me about the box.

And they never found the box when they looked in my house.

Then when it came to the nobbler glass, they said it was full of arsenic, and that I had been the only one who had filled the glass and given anything to my husband Michael to drink. They said this as though it were a crime for a wife to care for a sick husband. They said that I had fought with the constable when he wanted to take the glass as evidence, which I did not, or I do not remember doing, as I was in a very great sorrow at the time, and I may have been drowning my sadness. And others who were there have also said I did not fight with him, or that they did not see that I did, which is the same thing.

And in any case, if I had put arsenic in the nobbler glass, why would I have not thrown the glass away, before the constable even came there at all? There were plenty of those nobblers at the hotel, which is where the one I used to give Michael his last drinks on Earth had come from. I could have just nipped up to the hotel and got another. And with so many of these glasses about, how could the lawyer be certain that the glass shown as evidence in the trial was the same glass from my house?

They asked my little May if she seen the glass which was on display in the court, and pointed to the glass that sat on a table right in front of her in the courtroom. And they said it as though they wanted her to answer in a certain way. So, of course May, she said yes, she had seen that nobbler glass and it might have been the very same one which had sat beside Michael's bed. And that was exactly what the lawyer wanted her to say, so he smiled and thanked her, sure as you like, and said, No more questions, your Honour.

Even with May's story, the jury at the trial couldn't agree that I done it. And when they told the judge that they could not agree, the judge said they could go home, and so home they all went and that night they slept in their own beds.

But I got sent back to prison, to wait here while another

jury was found, and I had to sit through another trial with them talking as though I murdered Michael with Rough on Rats.

Then that second trial jury couldn't agree.

So the court went looking for another jury and sent me for another trial, although it was a different judge, and this time they charged me with murdering my first husband, Charles. My May came back into the court and gave her story, only this time they pestered her about the Rough on Rats and whether it was used to kill her own father and whether she had seen it before, when her father was alive, and she would have only been such a young thing then. She is still such a young thing. The trial courts are cruel to be doing this to my daughter and make her say her story at each trial, and even more so this time as they were saying it was her mother who killed her own father.

And cruel to me as well, for I have to listen each time.

The trial jury could not decide that I murdered Charles.

So the judge sent me back here.

And told me I am to wait while they find a new trial jury who says I done something to one of my husbands.

Brevities

In giving evidence against her mother, Louisa Collins, at the Central Criminal Court ... a pretty child, named May Andrews, 11 ½ years of age, was much affected. The prisoner and several of the jurors felt the situation keenly.

Evening News[3]

2.

Darlinghurst Gaol, Sydney

28 November 1888

This morning I wake early, before there's any light, and I grope my way to the slop bucket. I dip my hands in the water bucket which sits alongside the slops and I wash my face.

It is already hot and the cell is putrid with the smell of sweat and the privy bucket. I would like to sprinkle some water across the floor and lie there as it might afford some cool, but there is no room and if the warder comes and sees me lying down on the floor she would think I am mad.

I can hear little noise from outside the female cell block. The walls of the building are thick. There is always noise from within the walls, though. The warders, as they walk up and down the steps, the clanging of doors and the sounds from within the cells. In my cell there are just two beds made of straw mattresses placed on pieces of timber to keep them off the floor, a slop bucket, a water bucket and the small slit window. Some of the cells have four or five women in them, and the cells are no bigger than this one.

The air must be stifling.

Flora lies on the other bed in my cell and now I am awake her snoring makes it impossible to return to a state of sleep. She snores as though she has been down the hotel for the evening, gulping in her air with loud snorts, and then blowing it out with wobbling lips, making a ridiculous noise, one such as you make to entertain a baby by blowing bubbles at them. Between some of the breaths Flora holds the air, so the rhythm is not enough to hum you to sleep.

She cannot blame the drink for her snoring, as she has been locked away for six months for stealing and no drink has been available, at least none that she has shared with me. Flora does not protest her innocence, and freely admits to me that she has stolen and that she has been doing this profession since she was a girl. She likes the lice in prison, she says, and then she tips her head back and laughs, and when she does this you can see her black teeth.

She is due for release soon.

The flies are crawling over my skin, licking the little drops of moisture which sit there. There are so many flies that even though the morning is already warm, I keep the blanket over me to stop at least some of my body from being walked upon.

Flora's snoring reminds me of the house I had at Botany and all the children and men who lived there and how loudly some of the boarders snored.

When she is in the prison, Flora is always put to work in the prison laundry, her being a frequent visitor to the gaol. She says the warders know she can be trusted there, and has none who bear her a grudge and they don't worry she would push an inmate into the boiling water, or hit them in the back of the head with the washing dolly, as she says has happened with others in the past. She just cleans the linens and does not mind the heavy lifting, or the extra laundry when she is washing the private underthings for the warders.

Flora is wiry and strong. During the day, she soaks and boils and wrings and hangs, and so she comes back to our cell smelling fresh, which is a blessing in this small space, for there are those who share a cell with some who smell bad and who you can sniff out at the length of the dining table.

When they first put me in this cell, some months ago, the Superintendent of the Female Division – the Female Governor – was most polite and apologised that I must share with one who is convicted as though I might be booking into a hotel and asking for the best private room only to find it unavailable. I had a mind to say I was not booking into a hotel at all, but held my tongue. We do try not to put those who are here on remand in with prisoners, she said, but I must ask you share with one who is convicted of a crime because of the overcrowding. She treated me most civil and has always done, and it is a shame they do not have a woman such as the Female Governor in charge of the whole prison, for they are used to running large houses and men have no idea. Here, the Female Governor answers to the Prison Governor, just as a wife is supposed to answer to a husband, as the Prison Governor is a man and he is in charge of all of the cell blocks at Darlinghurst Gaol and not just the female cell block. He puffs out his chest at his grandness.

I was nervous of being in prison as I had no experience, but I've found Flora of great benefit. She knows her way around the women who are here, even though they come and go, and has told me who to be wary of and who can be trusted. She says there are women here who should rightly be in the lunatic asylum. Flora says the asylum takes only the worst of those with a madness as they have their own overcrowding, and so the women with only a little madness must stay here at the prison. She says it is as well that they stay here as conditions are very bad in the asylum, and I wonder how she would know such a thing, but I do not ask.

The warders shall come soon and open the door and the women will walk down the metal stairs with their slop pails, to empty them into the slop tubs in the exercise yard. A parade of piss, dearie, Flora calls it.

The 'clean' buckets, those which contain only night water, will go into one tub, and sit and fester to be used later in the laundry, as the ammonia is good for the linens. There is a warder to supervise the tipping of the buckets, but Flora says filth still makes its way into the laundry trough, and this is not pleasant to find in the wash.

The putrid slop buckets, those with filth, go into a separate tub – one of those is used by the women during the day – and the muck sits and stinks until cleared away by the male prisoners allocated to the night soil duties. There are so many women crowded in here that the smell from this area is as bad as one hundred privies, and the area is full of flies, and when you visit you must hold your breath and cover your nose, as much for the flies as the stink. While you sit, the flies cover your whole body.

I wait for the doors to open and the parade of piss to begin. My stomach growls, for after the parade will come breakfast.

We women take our meals in the exercise yard at long tables laid out for the purpose, although far too close to the slop tubs for my liking. There are always flies upon your food, particularly in summer. There are several hundred women crammed into this cell block and many hundreds more men in the cell blocks which are around us. All of us wanting feeding and waiting upon. The kitchen must never stop.

The prison meals are mainly of a mash variety and I suppose this to be as many of the prisoners do not have strong teeth. There is bread, hominy and watery stews, which are said to be meat and potatoes, but there is never much meat to be tasted.

At first I did not look at the other women, for fear of giving offence, but I do look upon most of them now and I have grown to like the meal times best of all. Until I came to prison, it had been a long time since I had sat and had a meal placed before me that was not one I had needed to prepare myself, so I like the experience of it, even if the meal is only prison food. There is something of a companionship among us, for we are a world of women all locked up together away from the men. And it is time out of our cells.

The warders allow the kitchen prison workers to give us a cup of tea, although they make sure this is lukewarm lest one of the prisoners throw it in the face of another to scald them, for Flora says there are those here who would. The prison kitchen is a distance away, so the tea is nearly cold when it comes. It is the worst tea you have ever tasted. On the first day it is so strong it might rip the flesh off your insides, and by the second day it is weaker, for the warders reuse the tea leaves for economies and after a few days it is simply dirty water.

Piss water, Flora says.

On the piss water days, the colour of the tea reminds me of the waters which used to run in the little creek near our home in Botany and I look into my cup and imagine I am there still, with the tea-trees down to the water's edge and the children playing in the shallows. I am grateful enough for my tea on any day, because I do not have to fetch the wood and pack the stove and light it and lug the water from the well and boil the pot myself. So I welcome the prison tea, even the piss water.

On Saturday afternoons the Church of England prisoners walk to the Chapel for the service. We women walk straight from the top level of the female cell block across a short walkway, high up off the ground, and we seat ourselves in the top part of the Chapel so that we sit above the men and they aren't distracted by our beauty. From that spot, we look down and see the many things the men do instead of listening to the chaplain's sermon. The chaplain is a quiet, gentle man. I like to listen to his sermons as they provide some distraction from my thoughts. In the past, I might have felt some joy considering all the men who sat below me in Chapel and imagining which I might prefer – which was the better looking, or which might best offer me protection from the world. But my present situation has cured me of such an interest.

In Chapel, notes are thrown up to sweethearts and I do not believe that the warders don't see this, for sometimes the throwers are none too quick. I have heard that the notes are all of the same type, confessing love.

I don't think the men care who finds such words, so long as it is a woman, even one of the female warders.

On most Sundays, we take our morning meal and then the Roman Catholics have their turn at Chapel, and there are so many of them there is a service on the Saturday besides. We sit in the exercise yard while a do-gooder woman, as Flora calls them, comes and sits on a chair on a platform and reads to us from a book of Sunday Bible readings.

I sit very still and I look, but I don't pay attention to the words the do-gooder reads. The words all sound the same in any case. I watch her. I look at the way she sits, the way she holds her head and her hands. She never lets you see any emotion while she reads. I want to learn to hold myself in this way in court to convince the judge to let me go.

I sit and practise how to hold myself as tight and stern as a do-gooder woman, and I give no one an opportunity to see inside me.

The warders come and sit in their chairs and watch. It passes the time for them to sit and they earn their wage just the same. Easy money for some.

Flora says the warders must protect any do-gooder who

comes, lest an inmate stab the woman or gouge her eyes. I have looked around and wondered which of us women would be the one to do such a thing.

I have not yet decided.

Maybe it would be me doing the gouging and stabbing.

After the reading, we have our dinner and then the prisoners are allowed to have visitors, and I have seen some of my children on occasion. It is hard for them to get here as they are scattered to the winds – the two older boys away from Sydney, working up near Newcastle somewhere, and the young ones must have someone to bring them. The police or the courts, I am not sure which, have separated my younger children and sent them out to live in different places. May is with someone who is appointed her guardian, although only temporary I am told, and I do not know if she lives with them in a house or in a children's home. I know Edwin and Charles are in a benevolent home, which I do not like, as this is something like an orphanage and they are not orphans.

I think Arthur and Frederick are still living in the house at Pople's Terrace.

Of course, I have also seen my children when they have testified in my trials, but these were not social visits.

When she comes to see me in prison, I do not want to quarrel with May over the words she said in court. She might not be brought back to see me if I do. So I hold myself back. Keep my emotions tight and try to speak of other things. But it is difficult to visit with your child in a place such as prison and so very hard to hear her testimony, and although I think she does not understand how damning her words are, I must still hear her say them.

The lawyers do not have much, but they have her words about the box of Rough on Rats and the glass she points out in court.

They have those things.

And my dead husbands.

Latest Special Telegrams

Louisa Collins, for the murder of her second husband, at Botany, will be tried the third time, at Darlinghurst ... the jury in previous trials having failed to agree.
The Maitland Mercury and Hunter River General Advertiser[4]

3.

Darlinghurst Gaol, Sydney

4 December 1888

I knew another trial was coming as Mr Lusk had told me to expect this, and now the Female Governor has been to tell me that my new trial will begin in the morning. She says to me that they will try me for the murder of my husband, so I ask which one, although I had thought it would be Michael.

Charles, she said, then she looked down at the paper in her hand and said, No, Mrs Collins, it is a trial for the murder of your husband Michael. She said she was sorry for making such a mistake.

I told her it was a simple mistake to make.

Flora has laundered my dress and my cape and they lie upon my mattress, there being nowhere to hang clothes in our cell. They don't let you have a nail in the wall on account of the injury you might do.

Flora has told me not to be worried, as three trial juries previous have not been able to reach a verdict and unless there is some new evidence this jury will no doubt think the same, even though they should be different men. She herself has heard much talk of my case.

She learns a lot from being in the laundry, for she says the warders do nothing when they are there but sit back on their arses and gossip. Lately, they say there has been much in the papers about me, although some not too kind neither, dearie. Flora has learnt to listen well as she cannot read very much and also it is useful in her profession, as she calls it, for she says conversation overheard is information which can be used, dearie.

In their gossip, the laundry warders nearly always speak of this warder or that one and complain about the wandering hands of the male warders and how they are no better than those they are sworn to guard. On occasion the warders say something and then think upon it as though they shouldn't have spoken and they ask Flora if she has heard. What do you think of that then, Flora, they call, and though she hears them, she always waits until they call a second time. And even then, she is slow to turn around so as to give the impression she has been thinking of other matters, or of a place miles away and only lately distracted from her thoughts. Flora says this is the best way to listen to gossip, and is the same way used by servants in the big houses, for she says she has been one of those, and you would not believe what she has heard. At other times, in the laundry, she also pretends she is going deaf, which she says they accept readily because of her age.

They lock us in the cells at five o'clock and it is a thing I do not like, the closed door. The door of my house at Botany was nearly always open and I would place a rock in front of it so it would not bang shut. The open door let in the air; with so many people in the house the odours could be none too pleasant.

We are locked up for so long and the window in my cell gives no air.

My neighbour at one time, Mrs Malone, did not ever leave her door open on account of the snakes, for she said she was from Ireland, where there were no snakes and a thank you to Saint Patrick for that. Snakes are the work of the devil to be sure, Louisa, she would say. And I told her that I was afeared of snakes too, but I had grown up in the bush and I knew that snakes would come into your house whether the door was open or not.

I think back to Mrs Malone, with these prison doors always being shut, and how I would like to tell her I was right. See, I would say, even when the strongest doors are shut the snakes can still get you, only these snakes will say you killed your husbands, for not all snakes crawl on their bellies, Mrs Malone.

When we are locked in our cells at night, Flora comes and lies next to me upon my straw mattress and she whispers to me and though her breath is foul because of her rotten teeth, I press my ear close to her mouth. I know she will not speak any louder as she does not want it learnt about her eavesdropping and even though we are locked in our cell a warder might be just outside the door without us knowing. She tells me more of the murderer in London, who is taking a knife to prostitutes and leaving their bodies all over the city, and it is a most dreadful thing which is happening and I am glad I am not there for the police cannot catch the man who is doing it. It is much discussed in the laundry as to who this man might be.

The warders talk of how I am called the Botany Murderess by some papers who do not like me, but other papers think the government is pursuing me by their keeping on with the trials, and there are those in high places who think it's wrong that I should be tried again and again.

Flora has said I should say my husbands beat me and that was why I done it, and they might let me off. She said I should complain about my solicitor, as one who was any good would not let me go to court so many times. But then, she said, he is appointed by the government and so he will make good money for being at so many murder trials as it is the murders which pay the best, or so she thinks.

Flora says some of the people who write to the papers say the men who are chasing after me are being wicked and only do so because I am a woman, and that these men are worried that all the wives in Sydney might want to get rid of their husbands with a bit of rat poison put into a cup of tea. And these men think that I should not be allowed to get away with it; I should be made an example of. Flora says she cannot remember if this is something that was written in the papers or something the warders said among themselves, but I say it is no matter for the thought would be the same.

She says there is a do-gooder woman who has written to the paper and said the courts should not be pursuing me as I have no vote, and I might be hung without any chance of 'parliamentary representation', although Flora says she is not entirely sure what this means. Flora thinks this is one of the do-gooders who read at the prison, but she cannot rightly remember the warders having said it was. And she says the talk then turned to whether women should be permitted the vote, or to keep their own children after their husbands might die, and that I should be careful when I get out of prison as there will be those who want to take my children away from me as I've no man to raise them, and no man will have me as I've killed my husbands. Then she adds that of course this will not be proven if I'm let out of gaol.

She says that she has heard this will be my last trial, for some men have said that if there is no conviction this time then they will have almost run out of juries in Sydney as there has been so much talk about my trials that it would not be fair to send me to court again. But, she says, if I am convicted I will need to hang, on account of the men and their cups of tea wanting me as an example.

We lie quiet for a moment.

Flora pats my arm and says I should not worry, they will not hang a woman, even though they used to do that in the mother country. There are those in this country who say it is wrong to watch a woman do the high-dance jig, and that is why there have been other women who have murdered and not been hung, just locked up for life, she says. And at any rate, Flora has been in gaol when they have done hangings but they've never done a woman in this gaol and she doesn't think the hangman would know how to do it to a woman, and she makes some rude gestures as she says this and she laughs.

I laugh too, but not really.

And we lie quiet for a time.

Then she pats my shoulder and says, Night, dearie, and gets up off my bed to use the slop bucket, as is her routine. She goes to her own mattress and I can soon hear her snoring, for although it is only early she is always tired after the laundering.

I think about everything Flora said. In the time we have shared a cell, she has never once asked me if I done for my husbands.

Darkness comes into the cell block and the warders light the candle sconces in the centre of the building, which they keep burning all night so they have light should there be trouble, as it would be too inconvenient to be lighting a candle should trouble come.

I lie and swat at the mites and think it must cost the government considerable money to keep candles burning all night in prison, and it might be cheaper for the government to hang a prisoner whenever they can.

Then I imagine a rope coming around my neck.

Intercolonial
(FROM OUR OWN CORRESPONDENTS)
NEW SOUTH WALES

Louisa Collins was again placed on her trial at the Central Criminal Court to-day for the murder of her husband, Michael Peter Collins, at Botany, in July last. On two former occasions the jury were unable to agree. The evidence is not yet concluded.

The Brisbane Courier[5]

4.

Darlinghurst Gaol, Sydney

5 December 1888

Today, I am to walk to the Darlinghurst Courthouse through the tunnel which leads there from inside the prison. They always have two warders escort me when I do this walk in case I make a run for it. I do run through the tunnel, if I can, to escape the rats.

Female warders escort me through the grounds of the prison, but the entrance gate to the tunnel is always guarded by a male warder.

When the door of my cell opens, it is Warder Harper who steps inside and I am glad. Warder Harper is tall and softly spoken. I know her first name to be Alice, and though I call her Warder Harper to her face, in my mind she is Alice.

Alice waits while I place my bonnet upon my head and tie the ribbon under my chin. Then again, while I place the light cloak about my shoulders and tie its ribbon. Having no looking glass, I turn my face to her to enquire whether my bonnet is straight and she gives a slight nod. This is a ritual we have performed before and though Alice doesn't often speak to me, as this is discouraged between warder and prisoner, I take comfort in her nod, and would like to think she wishes me well by ensuring my appearance is the best it may be.

She beckons me out of the cell and together we walk down the metal steps to the main entrance of the female cell block. We go to the female cell block warder's office and Alice signs in the large book to say that she's taking me to court, and then we walk through the main double doors.

A few of the female prisoners are in the exercise yard and they pause in their circular walk to call out good luck to me before they are quietened by the warders who guard them.

The female prisoners take an interest in my trials. Flora says they've never heard of someone being tried so many times for the same crime, and they say that I am treated unfairly because I am a woman. But what woman is not treated unfairly? The Queen perhaps? She can do what she likes and has all the money she wants, and it does her no good, for you never see her smile, even though she sits with the big crown on her head and all the diamonds around her neck.

It's not diamonds they want to put around *my* neck.

Alice places a hand lightly on my arm as we walk out of the world of women. We go past the bathhouse and the men's hospital wing. The hospital wing has larger windows as fresh air is considered beneficial to illness. Some of the men stare out at us from behind the bars.

We turn past the hospital building and see the male warder who is to open the tunnel gate for us and take us through to the court. It is Warder Crisp and I hear a small sigh come from Alice's lips, for this man is none too pleasant.

He is large and heavy and has the bulbous red nose of one who likes his drink and a neck which bulges over the top of his collar and a belly that puts a strain on his uniform buttons.

He is one of those men who thinks he is still in his youth and considers himself a charmer. He is not.

As we approach, he gives a smirking grin and he says, I'm here to take charge of the virtues of my lovelies, and what lovelies we have.

Alice and I say nothing.

I've the keys to happiness right here, he says, then he waves a hand to the area near his belt, which might mean he is pointing to the keys that dangle there, or that he's pointing to something else. I feel Alice's hand tense.

He leans in towards Alice and says, If you give me a kiss I'll open the gate for you. Alice takes a small step towards me and reaches her spare hand to the watch pinned to her uniform. She looks down and checks the time.

She says nothing.

I lower my eyes. Crisp continues talking at Alice, and it is as though he does not see me there. We stand for a moment. Him waiting for his kiss and Alice with her hand resting on my arm, waiting for the gate to open.

She checks the time upon her watch again, and he loses some of his bluster. He knows that Alice will have signed me out and there may be some explaining to do if he delays much longer. Then he grunts and mutters as he turns and unlocks the gate. Alice removes her hand from my arm and gestures me down the steps and we begin to hurry along the tunnel. I think she has quickened her pace to avoid the gaoler, who is fumbling at the steps to lock the heavy gate behind him, but perhaps it is because of the rats.

It's not so very far in the dark underground to the courthouse and I am glad of it. This particular tunnel is only a short one, although I have used the longer tunnel which runs from under the Governor's mansion. I have seen rats scurrying through each of these tunnels for they are exactly the types of places where rats like to live.

I don't want the rats to jump on me. Evil creatures.

Today I see but one rat, who runs ahead of us through a large puddle, making a little wave in the water as he goes, then he runs up the wall. I cross to the other side of the tunnel, although it's not so very wide as to be beneficial and I fear the rat might still be able to jump across and onto me. Alice crosses with me and we hurry, single file, through the section where the rat will be sitting high on the wall and ready to pounce.

We step through the puddles as best we can and lift our skirts to avoid the hems getting wet. I hear the guard behind us call something, but neither Alice nor I pay heed. There's a lit candle halfway along the tunnel and a brighter one at the other end, which is the gate to the Darlinghurst Courthouse.

There are steps leading up to the courthouse gate, and an officer is waiting on the outer side. Alice and I pause for Crisp to catch up, which he does, red in the face and puffing. The officer looks at the fat gaoler with disdain, and holds this look while Crisp fumbles with his keys and opens the lock. Alice and I enter the courthouse and Crisp locks the gate again and disappears down the tunnel.

I hope the rat finds him.

There's more signing of books and then I'm led to a courthouse cell where I sit until I'm called. Alice sits in the cell alongside me, as she is to protect my dignity while I'm in court, such dignity as I have, being charged with murder.

We sit for but a moment and then my name is called and we walk up the narrow steps to the special box which is allocated for the prisoner. 'Defendant' the name says on the front of the box, but Alice sits in the box alongside me and she is not on trial, and so I think the name is wrong. There are special boxes for each of the different people who come to court and each of these has a name written upon it: one box each for police, witnesses, jurors and prospective jurors, and another large box for the press.

The public sit up behind me in the court on a terrace area where there is seating, much as in a theatre, which is right, I suppose, for we are playing our part in the theatre of the court. My case has caused much excitement in Sydney, and if what Flora overhears is true, there are more discussions in the papers on a daily basis. When I go to my various trials, the courtroom is always full with those who have come to see the entertainment.

I am always the first to go into one of the special boxes. They like the defendant secure before the others arrive.

When Mr Lusk comes in, he looks in my direction and nods, but does not come over to speak with me. I would like to ask him why I'm being tried again, what new evidence they have found, but he gives me no opportunity, for he turns and speaks with the other lawyer and I see them bow their heads together. They are so close that their curly wigs touch.

During the first trial Mr Lusk seemed in some discomfort in the courtroom, but now he has had the opportunity to become familiar and so he prances quite confidently and argues my case and says M'Lord just as well as the rest of the lawyers who speak in the court.

The doors open and the public and the pressmen come in.

I see the pressmen jostle for their seats and I can hear the public behind me as they scramble.

Some call out to me, but there will be nothing new to be heard, and so I try not to listen. Give us a smile Louisa, burn in hell Louisa Collins, murdering bitch, whore, slut. There will not be a kind word among them.

The bailiff will make no effort to quieten them until we all have to rise for the judge.

I keep my bonnet on as it gives me some protection from their words, and the opportunity to peer about me. The men who write their papers all perch on a long bench to the side of the court. A bunch of old crows upon a sheep-fence rail.

They are no better than the tom cats who call for the females at night, making up any sort of a song to attract attention. There is one in particular who never seems to write anything down. He has the look of a drunk about him, that one.

The others sit ready with their pencils held above their paper, and they stare at me, bold as you like. I try to hold myself tight and firm, like a do-gooder woman, but perhaps I should cry as it might be tears they want to see.

When a time has passed, I remove my bonnet and this starts a new round of insults and whistles, then I remove my cape, and place both beside me on my seat, smoothing the cape as I put it down.

Then I put my hands upon the small table in front of me and wait until the judge enters.

As I do these things, I turn slightly in my seat and I sneak a look at those in the gallery. I see those who wish me well and those who wish me ill, and it is the ones who wish me ill who take the greatest delight in the proceedings. Some of them take their place on the stand and damn me. I should like to damn them back.

We are told to rise and then when the judge comes in, he sits upon his throne. He has a canopy over his head, and on the wall behind him there is a carving of a lion and another animal pulling a shield between them. It doesn't matter which judge or which trial, for they all look the same. The judge wears the biggest wig of all. This one looks as though he has just finished having breakfast with the Queen and a tiny piece of bread was left between his teeth, for he rolls his tongue around while he listens as though he is trying to work this piece out of the gap.

He is well pleased with himself.

I have been in my trial courts many times and I know the judge and lawyers do not want to hear a word I might say. They just keep talking among themselves and bringing in their witnesses and my children and doing their show for the new jury. I told my story at the inquest and it was written down but I was only halfway through and I did not finish. Now at the trials they do not ask me to speak. They just read out my statement each time.

The second inquest tried to find out how my first husband Charles Andrews and my baby John Collins had died. The men of the inquest court, they did not leave my husband and tiny baby to rest in their graves, the same graves they had lain in for some time previous. No, they dug up the bodies and pulled them apart. And then they took great delight in telling the court all about how the bodies were.

When the doctor spoke of my baby, he talked as though it was not a baby he looked at at all. He might have found some leftover stew in a pot, with the fat curdled on the bones and nothing remaining but a small amount of gristle in the gravy, and maggots. There are always those in leftovers.

There was much made of what was found in the baby's coffin, for it had been sitting in water, I believe. They spoke of the muck, what was there, how what was found was put in a jar, and I did not know there could be so much discussion of what might be held within a small body.

They should've shown some decency and left him be.

They took his little body from the ground and cut him open, pulling out his insides and whatnot. John was not ever more than a small baby anyway, and he never did thrive, so I imagine there was not much left of him to be pulled apart, for the worms would have taken their share.

What shall become of the things from his body? Do they stay sitting in a jar somewhere on a shelf, like bottled peaches?

And all of their pulling apart of my child did them no good, for the jury at the inquest said that my baby John had died of natural causes.

If they had asked me, I would have told them that.

News of the Day

LOUISA COLLINS was again placed upon her trial at the Central Criminal Court yesterday for the alleged murder of her husband, Michael Peter Collins, at Botany, on the 8th of July last. The Bench was occupied by his Honor the Chief Justice. The case was conducted on behalf of the Crown by Mr. Heydon. The defence of the accused was again undertaken by Mr. Lusk, at the request of his Honor. A number of witnesses were examined during the day; but the case for the Crown had not concluded when the Court adjourned at half-past 5 o'clock. The jury were locked up for the night.

The Sydney Morning Herald[6]

Central Criminal Court
The Alleged Murder at Botany

The trial of Louisa Collins, for the alleged murder of her husband, Michael Peter Collins, at Botany, on the 8th of July last, was continued ...

Dr. Martin was again called, and gave further evidence with regard to the postmortem examination. He deposed that if arsenic was present in Andrew's body at the time of his death the water in the coffin when the body was exhumed would have tended to dissolve it; he quoted cases in which no trace of arsenic had been found in the body after death, although it was known that the deceased had died from arsenical poisoning ...

A number of witnesses who were called at the previous trials gave evidence, some of them to the effect that they had visited Collins's during his illness, and had seen the accused waiting upon him and giving him certain liquids to drink ...

The statement of the accused made at the inquest was read to the jury ...

John Walker, a carter, deposed that he worked with Collins at the woolwashing establishment; on the last day on which Collins was at work he was taken sick, and witness had to do his work for him; they were at Rookwood, and were engaged in carting skins; Collins was taken suddenly ill, and had to go into the bush, and witness loaded the skins for him ...

Mr. Lusk, in addressing the jury on behalf of the accused, said they had now for three days been listening to the evidence in this very important case. They had listened to a very large amount of testimony as to fact and as to opinion, and it was now his duty to assist them as far as he could ... in coming to a conclusion upon a most difficult and important case – a case in which was involved the life of a human being and the wellbeing of society ...

Because it had been shown that the accused could have administered the poison, that was no reason for finding her guilty of murder ...

The police visited the house and gave the accused every warning, so that if she was guilty and knew there was arsenic in the tumbler of milk, what would have been easier than for her to have disposed of the contents of the glass? ...

Mr. Heydon addressed the jury at some length on behalf of the Crown ... He submitted that the whole of the evidence pointed to only one conclusion, and that was that the accused was guilty of the murder of her husband ...

The Court adjourned at 10 minutes to 8 o'clock.

The Sydney Morning Herald[7]

5.

Darlinghurst Gaol, Sydney

7 December 1888

It is late and the court is only just finishing.

Today has been the same stories from the other trials and talk of how both my husbands died. There is nothing new among the stories except that they are made bigger with each telling. One witness remembers more gossip each time she takes the stand, and flutters and preens with the excitement of it.

I am on trial for murdering Michael, but the lawyers have been talking of Charles and how they dug up his body and what they found when they did.

Someone said he knew a case where there was no arsenic in a body when it was dug up, but it was known the man was killed by arsenic. So what does it matter that they find arsenic with their tests or if they find none at all; they suppose I killed Charles all the same. But this trial is for murdering Michael, so I do not know why they are even talking of Charles on any account. They are just wanting to tell the jury I done it to a husband before, most likely.

Some of the witnesses have given evidence time and time again, at both inquests and each of the trials. The doctor, the one who gives the evidence about the bodies, he did not seem to take kindly to being called for another trial.

I suppose it is not convenient for that sort of doctor to have to stop his work and come to court again and read his words from his notebook. He would not like to keep his dead bodies waiting.

Alice and I walk back through the tunnel this evening and Warder Crisp is again our escort. He is waiting in the tunnel when the officer brings Alice and me down, direct from the court. Because the hour is late, the tunnel is very dark, and I can't see the rats. While Crisp locks the gate, Alice and I hurry along, but as we near the steps at the other end Crisp pushes himself between us and he speaks very badly to Alice; there is no escaping his nasty tongue.

We see a light. The Female Governor stands behind the gate at the top of the stairs and I think she has heard Crisp's words for she is scowling. Crisp fumbles finding the key to the gate. By her lamp, I see he has gone red in the face, but it may be from his exertions.

The Female Governor barks at Warder Crisp that he may walk behind and follow us to the female cells, given the lateness of the hour. We women walk quickly. I hear Crisp's wheezing as he tries to keep up with us.

When we reach the big doors at the entrance of the female cell block the Female Governor turns and dismisses Crisp. She opens the doors with her own keys and we enter. Alice signs me in at the office and the Female Governor tells me there is dinner waiting for me in the exercise yard as I have missed the evening meal. Alice and I head to the long tables, and I eat from the bowl that has been left for me. The food is now cold, but it is there and put before me and so I eat.

Alice sits on the chair and she wrings her hands in her lap. I look at her and she looks back at me. We do not speak.

Then Alice walks me to my cell and locks me in. I use the slop bucket, and speak to Flora, who has woken and asks how the day has gone as though I have been on an outing to the seaside. I begin to tell her when there is a key in the door of the cell, and the door is opened by Alice and behind her is the chaplain, Canon Rich.

I bend my head to smooth my dress.

He says a few words of greeting to Flora, and she steps up from her bed and speaks with him.

Then he turns to me and the slop bucket is in the corner and I have just finished using it and the smell in this summer heat is none too pleasing. I am barely accustomed to it myself.

He takes a handkerchief from his pocket and places it upon his nose, making a small noise as though he is about to sneeze, but I think he is trying to mask his displeasure at the smell.

So I play along with his game, and wait for his sneeze to happen.

He makes a pretence of wiping his nose.

Good evening, Mrs Collins, he says.

And I say, Evening, sir.

You had a long day in court, he says.

I think of watching my May in the witness box.

Yes, it was a long day. I nod again. Yes, sir.

And how did this day go for you, do you think? Does the matter progress in your favour?

I give a shrug. I could not say, sir.

He nods. No doubt you are tired after the day, he says. Well, I shall let you get your rest, Mrs Collins, and I shall call on you again tomorrow. And he gives a little prayer for Flora and me and we stand still and listen to his words.

The slop bucket smells.

He finishes his prayer and then he steps from our cell into the corridor and Alice shuts and locks the metal door. I hear them murmuring together as they walk away and, though I press my ear to the door, I cannot make out what it is they are saying.

The Botany Murder Case
Extracts from the Murderess's Letters

It's the jury, and some good and some bad wishers. I will not be so wicked as to think they are not some that has common feeling in them for to see me in such a sad, deplorable position; and, above all, I am compelled to sit and see my only daughter, that is just 11 years old the 17th of October. I am the mother that has nourished and cherished her from her birth. In fact, many a time I thought I could not rear her. Being the only daughter, my heart and soul was wrapped up in her, and I hear her, I see her, before my eyes, made to stand in a witness-box, with a book in her right hand, and she takes her oath, and she says, of course, she knows the nature of an oath, and says sufficient to take her own poor mother to the gallows, and gives her evidence in such a straightforward manner that the words belong to another head and another mouth of some wicked and inhuman pieces of iniquity quite unfit to walk the earth …

Evening News[8]

The Botany Poisoning Cases
Mrs Collins Sentenced to Death

After the failure of two trials in the case of the death of the second husband and one in the case of the first husband a conviction has at last been recorded against Louisa Collins for the murder by arsenical poisoning of her second husband, Michael Peter Collins, at Botany in July, 1888. The last trial, which has extended over several days at the Central Criminal Court, was concluded yesterday afternoon, when the jury, after a retirement of two hours, returned a verdict of guilty. The Chief Justice, in passing sentence, said the verdict was the only one that could reasonably have been arrived at. The murder was one of most peculiar attrocity, as day by day the prisoner had watched the man whom above all others she ought to have loved and cherished die slowly from the effects of the poison she had given him without showing the least mercy. There was too much reason to suppose that Andrews (the prisoner's first husband) had also met his death at the prisoner's hands, and that she had watched his death to the same way as she had done that of Collins. It would be cruel for him (the Chief Justice) to hold out the least hope of a reprieve to the prisoner. Mrs Collins, who throughout the several trials has displayed great callousness, heard the sentence of death pronounced in the same unmoved manner.

The South Australian Advertiser[9]

6.

Darlinghurst Gaol, Sydney

8 December 1888

Shackles are placed about my wrists and ankles as I sit in the defendant's box. I look down at them and see these are someone else's hands, someone else's feet. Where are my own?

Alice is not with me today. What is she doing, why is she not here?

I stand. Two warders take hold of my arms.

I slip at the bottom of the steep steps which lead down from the defendant's box. My dress catches on the shackles. I can't see my bonnet, where has it gone?

I stumble into a tunnel; it is these legs now, they aren't walking properly.

We come out of the tunnel and I am taken to a different part of the gaol, to the building near the main gate; perhaps the men will open the gates and remove the shackles and I will be free.

But we turn and walk into a room and they tell me to sit.

I sit.

I can see out of the window. There is the building which

has a skull and crossbones above the door. The mortuary. Flora has told me this is where the gaol dead are brought and doctors are allowed to poke and prod, the dead being unable to say no. I would never have thought such a place could exist, but now I have heard the terrible stories of what they did to my husband Charles and my baby John, and them not being freshly dead. I had not known such evil lived in the world.

A photographer comes in and sets up his equipment. He says he will take a photograph of me. I think the gaol must have brought him in special to do so.

Why do they want another photograph? They have one from when I first came to gaol.

I look back out of the window. Will they hang me? Will they really hang me? And then lay me in that mortuary so they can poke and prod and measure? Will parts of me be put in a jar somewhere, or a cast made of my head?

They take my photograph. I do not have the right hands and feet and I am not wearing my bonnet.

I do not think the photograph will be of me.

I hear the warders say that my being sentenced to hang will be a great inconvenience to the gaol, as I will not be able to be placed in the condemned cells on account of them being in the male wing and I need female warders to attend me.

The Female Governor comes into the room and says if this business is concluded then I need to be taken to the female cell block, for arrangements have been made there. The warders take hold of my arms again and we walk behind the Female Governor, me shuffling and clinking along in the chains.

Everything has changed.

They said I done it.

They said I should have no hope.

They said I should hang.

When we reach the female cell block, we do not go up the stairs to the second floor, to the cell I share with Flora. We stay on the ground floor and head to the far end of the block, to a different cell. It is a big cell, but there is only one bed and so I do not know where Flora will sleep.

The bed is on the floor. There is a blanket on top of the mattress and a prison gown and cap lie upon it. There is a slop bucket and a water bucket in one corner and a chair in the other. The slit of a window has no bars, as the opening is too small to climb through. The floor is sandstone and it is wet. I think it has only just been washed. And I think the mattress will rot if it sits on the wet floor for any length of time.

The Female Governor points to the shackles on my wrists and legs. The warder takes the key from her pocket and undoes these, then tells me to remove my cape.

I cannot undo the tie.

It is because these are not my hands. They are the hands of someone who murdered Michael.

They cannot undo the ribbon.

It is the Governor herself who steps forward and loosens the ribbon.

I remove the cape and then the warder tells me to remove my dress. She holds out the black prison gown and cap. I fumble and take a great deal of time.

I place my dress and cape upon the bed. I will need to find my bonnet.

I put on the prison gown and cap.

The Female Governor is speaking and she says I am to have a warder with me at all times.

The warder shall sit upon the chair in the corner.

Why, ma'am? I ask, though it is not my voice which says this.

To keep you safe, she says.

The Female Governor looks about the cell and nods to the warder. Then she turns and leaves and locks the door behind her, leaving the warder. I see her now, it is Warder Anderson in the cell with me.

Warder Anderson walks to the chair and sits upon it, then she stretches out her legs and folds her arms across her chest. She looks at me and I do not know what to do under her gaze.

I sit upon the bed and look at the hands before me.

They have become mine again.

I feel my feet, my ears, touch my throat.

It is all me.

I am real.

7.

I lie down and turn my face to the wall and cry silent tears. I cannot be sure how long I lie upon the bed.

There is the sound of the key turning in the lock.

Warder Anderson is still sitting on the chair and she stands as Alice enters with a bowl and a wooden spoon. She says to Anderson that she is there to relieve her duty and that Anderson is free to go out into the prison. Anderson looks to Alice and nods, although I imagine sitting on a chair is more inviting work than some of the other chores.

They exchange the key and Anderson locks Alice in the cell with me.

Here, Louisa, she says, I have brought some dinner for you. Alice is as calm and as casual as you like, and I think I must have had a bad dream and that is why Anderson was in the cell.

I look about me and see the cell is not my own, and I look down and see I wear a prison dress.

Then I remember.

8.

Alice motions for me to sit on the chair and I rise from the bed and do so, taking the bowl of food from her.

She bends and pats my bed, fluffing the area where I have lain, tucking the blanket in over the sacking. She smooths the blanket almost tenderly and as I watch her do this I feel myself about to cry.

I place a hand over my eyes.

I hear the rustle of Alice's skirts and she is beside me; a firm hand squeezes my shoulder.

She tells me not to be discouraged, that she will keep me company for the evening, and that I should eat up before my dinner goes cold.

It is not like her to chatter.

I eat.

They found me guilty because of a nobbler glass, and a box, and because of the words of my child.

I force the food down.

A glass.

A box.

My daughter.

I do not finish my dinner.

I put the bowl down and go back to the bed. Alice takes her place upon the chair. We neither of us say anything.

Some time later, for it is now dark, there is a key in the door and the Female Governor comes into the room and says a visitor wishes to see me and I am to come out of my cell. She is carrying shackles and motions to Alice to place the irons upon my hands and feet, which Alice does.

My hands look different in these shackles, and again I think they are not my own. It is as though being in irons has made me a new person. I am now a woman who has done a terrible thing.

But it was not me who done it. It was the woman who wears the black prison gown and shackles, and that is why these hands are not mine.

The Female Governor and Alice lead me through the cell block to the heavy wooden doors. They write in the book and then we cross a gravel path and head towards the Chapel.

We go into a room on the bottom floor of the Chapel. I did not know this room existed; I thought the men's bathhouse was under the Chapel, for that is what Flora has said. I have only ever been to this building by crossing the walkway from the female cell block.

This room has only one straight wall, the main wall curving all around like half a circle, in keeping with the round shape of the building.

There is a table, and the prison chaplain, Canon Rich, is bending over it as I enter. Through the material of his jacket I can see his shoulder blades; they are sharp and thin.

He turns, having heard the clinking of my chains, and he winces when he sees me shackled.

Surely there is no need for this? he asks the Female Governor.

It is the regulations, Chaplain, she says. Now, at any time when Mrs Collins is to be moved around the prison she is to be attired like this.

And can these not be removed when she is in the sanctity of the Chapel? he asks.

They may not, she says.

Canon Rich looks at me. Welcome, Mrs Collins, he says.

Welcome yourself, I think, although I am glad to see him.

He motions for me to sit upon one of the chairs. I shuffle to the chair and Alice helps me to sit, on account of my being unable to use these chained hands.

All is well, Governor, he says. You may leave us in the care of your warder here.

The Female Governor hesitates and then says that is as well for there is much to be done.

He smiles at her and she turns and leaves, then he beckons to Alice to sit upon the bench at the side of the room.

I look around me. There are three candles and they are all lit. They throw a gentle light across the sandstone.

A Bible sits upon the table.

Canon Rich turns to me. Are you well, Mrs Collins? he says.

I think it is an odd question to ask someone who has just had the death sentence passed upon them, but I do not say this. Instead, I merely answer him as he would expect.

I am very well, sir, I say.

Very good, very good, he says.

I am thinking he will next ask me of the trial and the verdict and to confess my sins, but he does not. He asks something completely different.

I have enjoyed the little talks we have had in the past, he says, although you have never told me of where you grew up.

I do not see how this matters on any account, but I say, No, sir.

It was not in Sydney, I think?

No, sir.

Ahh, he says.

I feel I have passed some sort of a test by knowing where it was that I grew up. I can hear by his voice that he is trying to create a friendship between us. I have leant against enough pub walls to know when a man is trying to make friends with you. Seeking to force an intimacy, my mother would say.

The chaplain is not looking at me now; he has turned to face the curved wall of the room and examines the brickwork, poking his finger at the sandstone as though it is the first time he has seen a piece of rock.

I see you in church, he says.

Here it comes, I think.

Yes, sir, I say.

You love the Lord? he says.

This is the test, soon he will ask me how many verses I know of the Bible, how often I go to church; it is always the same with the men of the cloth, they like to hear a good report card, or perhaps even a bad one as then they may fix it. Well, he knows I go to church regular since I have been here, for all the prisoners have to. So perhaps he won't ask that one. I know what he expects me to say and so I say it.

Yes, sir, I say. I do.

He nods. Again, I have got it right. But then, I would hardly say different to a chaplain.

He says nothing for a moment; he is like one of the men in court, pausing before each question.

When you were a child, he says, were you baptised?

I wait, playing his pausing game.

I think so, sir, although I cannot remember it.

Of course, he says and gives a gentle smile.

Do you think of your parents? he says.

I do not understand why he is asking me of my parents. His questions are all over the place; there is no reason to them, talking of church and where I was born and my parents. I think there must be some scheme to his questions. Perhaps he is being like one of the lawyers, asking his questions, trying to catch out a lie. I do not answer straight away, then I say, I think of my mother, sir, and I write to her, but my father has passed on.

I see, he says.

Then the chaplain runs his hand over the piece of sandstone, turns and steps to the table, pulling out a chair and making a loud scraping noise as he does so.

I should like to know more about you, Mrs Collins, he says. I would like to know more of your life before. He waves a hand, at nothing in particular, but I take it to mean before prison. I only know of you from here, he says, and I am sure there is much more of you to know.

Why do you want to know, sir?

I am interested, he says. I think I might be able to help you and prepare you if I know you better and it might be of benefit to you to think of – here he pauses – other things. It might distract you from the trying times ahead of us.

I lower my head at this.

Prepare me? Prepare *me*? Does he have trying times ahead of him? Have the words of his only daughter been used to convict him? Has he been sentenced to death this very day and told to hold out no hope for mercy and to seek out a minister to prepare him?

Mrs Collins, he says.

I look up.

He leans forward in his chair and looks at me intently. It will help if we consider happier times, he says, if we can talk of events other than the sad situation in which we find ourselves.

Happier times? I think. What are they to me? When have I had happier times? I was most recently happy with Michael, but I cannot think of him now without a great sadness coming over me. I was happy when I was a carefree girl with my family, and when I was in Merriwa. I was happy when I held my new-born babies. But I have been laid low with all my troubles.

For the moment, you should think of the times when you have been most happy, for these times will be of comfort to you, Canon Rich tells me.

I try to believe him.

9.

I am not by rights a natural-born storyteller, although when I have had some beer in me, or a swig of gin, or even a little brandy, I have been known to sing, which is like telling a story, I suppose. But there will be no hope of alcohol coming to me in prison and I have little enough to sing about here.

A nip of courage would make it easier for me to speak, although perhaps it is better to have my wits about me, as when I gave my very first statement to the constable I had been sipping beer and could not remember my story.

I realise I have been thinking for some time, and when I look up, the chaplain is quietly watching me. He has his elbows on the table and his chin resting on his hands. Alice is focused on her fingers, examining one of her nails. They are both waiting for my story to commence.

I look down at my chains. Today I have been whipped and now I am tied up as a punishment.

The chaplain gives me a tiny smile and then he begins to talk of his own life and of his own growing up.

He tells me of his parents, and how they came to the colonies for a new start and to provide a warmer climate for his mother, as this had been recommended by the doctors for the bad cough she had at the time.

Did the warmer climate help her? I ask.

He says nothing, but he looks down.

I do not ask more.

But he tells me some of his story regardless and of his childhood after his mother died. This story might be one which he has often told prisoners, as a way of softening them into speaking with him, for there is no faster way to create a companionship with a person than to speak gently of your mother, or so has been my understanding. He probably has this one ready for condemned prisoners. It might not even be a true story – I have no way of knowing – but then, he is a man of God and so would not lie. I feel I should return his story with one of my own.

I think carefully about how much I should tell him, how might the chaplain hurt me with whatever I say to him, and then I decide there might not be more to be done, for being condemned to die is surely one of the worst places a person might find themselves. I perhaps do not have much time to think of what I should tell him. The government will hang me soon if they can and telling him my story might help me. A few lines about his own mother is not worth much, but perhaps they are worth a start.

I am one of those people who can remember their life from when they were very young, sir, I say.

One of my first memories is sitting on the lap of my sister Elizabeth on the bench outside our small cabin, in the dark.

Even as I speak of it I believe I can smell honey, for when the wattle is flowering there is nothing like it for the smell of honey in the air.

My sister was rocking me on her lap, I tell him, and we were looking up to see the stars. Elizabeth was telling me a story about the stars and Heaven, and though she was only five years older than me, she was like a mother to me, as is often the way with big families, for if there is an older girl in the family she cares for the rest of the brood and helps out her own mother, and so it was for Elizabeth.

Do you still visit with your sister Elizabeth?

I shake my head. Oh no, sir, we have not visited with each other for these many years and we have gone our separate ways as grown women, as you do when you get older. But I always think of her fondly. She was the kindest of sisters when we were children.

And even as I tell him this story of my life, I wonder if it is true. I cannot be sure this is the earliest memory I have, because childhood memories can come in layers, and they can trip you up and then when you add something to the story later you think that part of the memory was there all along. And I have seen the layers of memory at work, most recently, with people thinking back upon things and changing their recollections and adding in words. And not all of those people children neither.

There were many times when I was a child that we sat outside on the bench and I was held by Elizabeth and the air smelt of honey, so I cannot be sure that this time was the first, but I tell him it was anyway.

I am given to thinking he understands I am not telling him the whole story.

10.

The other warder does not come to escort me. Perhaps the prison has forgotten me, or is not used to the routine of having a condemned woman in the gaol.

The chaplain prays over me and then it is just Alice and I who walk back to my new cell. I would not be able to run away, regardless; these chains make it hard to even walk. The stars tonight are lovely. They make me think of my father, as he learnt to read the stars, but perhaps I think of him because of the story I have just told.

I walk back to my cell comforted.

Talking of my childhood memories has taken me from the horror of being condemned and flown me to my youth, which I suppose was the chaplain's intention.

I sleep well, in spite of the events of the day, or perhaps because of them, for there is nothing like hearing your life will soon end to tire you out. I dream of trees flowering and of pastures of wheat and flocks of sheep, and when I wake, I believe I can smell honey again.

It is not honey. It is the smell of the prison.

Alice had been sitting on the chair when I fell asleep, but when I wake there is another warder, one I have not seen before, sitting there.

She has her head leant back against the wall. She is asleep. There must have been a change of guard through the night, although I did not hear the heavy door of the cell opening. This warder is very thin and spare and looks quite severe, even while sleeping. Her thin black hair is parted in the middle and pulled back tightly behind her ears and she has a bony face and a long pointed nose, which curves downwards to a sharp point. In her black warder's uniform she has the appearance of being a witch.

She is sleeping so soundly that I could hit her on the head with my slop bucket if I wanted.

I don't.

I stand from the mattress, and lift the skirt of my gown over the slop bucket and relieve my morning water. The sound wakes the warder and she opens her eyes to see her charge pissing into the bucket.

She does not look away.

When I finish, I go to the water bucket to drink and wash my face. Then I return to my bed, lie down and roll over to face the wall.

Later, I hear the women of the prison with their slop buckets, clattering down the stairs.

A warder comes to empty mine.

I find the procession of piss strangely comforting.

The Catholic prisoners would be heading to church this morning, it being Sunday.

Would they know, I wonder, that I have been convicted, that the jury said I done it? Or might they think that I am released, that another jury could not make up their mind and so this time the court set me free? Flora would know I have gone somewhere, as I was not in her cell. If she does not yet know the details, she will hear soon enough, as the warders will gossip in the laundry tomorrow.

Over the clink of the buckets and the sound of the footsteps upon the stairs, I hear a call from within the walls of the cell block: Chin up, dearie.

Flora.

The warder still has not spoken. There is noise outside and the door is unlocked and Alice comes into the cell, carrying a small chair with her.

Good day to you, Warder Bryce, she says and nods.

I am here to relieve you of your duties, she says, so that you may bring the prisoner some food.

Then Alice turns to me. And I am bringing you a chair, Mrs Collins, she says, that you may have somewhere to sit instead of being required to be on your bed all day, and she gives me a small smile, just a tiny lifting of the corner of her lips, but I see it all the same.

I am grateful as there is something undignified about lying near to the floor while another person sits on a chair, although perhaps it is the fact they sit in a higher position to you, like a king upon a throne, or a judge upon his bench.

And, of course, on the floor, there are always the rats to consider.

Alice places the chair down and I get up from the bed and sit upon it.

I feel much improved.

Warder Bryce brings me my breakfast. Watery porridge and a cup of strong tepid tea. New tea leaves for Sunday, I think. I am not allowed to go and listen to the do-gooder read. From my cell, I hear the noise she makes, but I cannot make out the words.

All that effort to hold myself tight in court, like her. I might as well have howled and screamed and fainted.

Being tight did me no good. The newspapers said I was cold and heartless.

Sunday afternoon is the time when visitors are allowed to come to the gaol, and though I wait and hope in earnest, that afternoon none come. I am bitterly disappointed, for I desire to see the children, even more so after my terrible sentence. And if they are to come and visit, they will come on a Sunday.

I say this to Alice and she says I should not fret, as she has been told by the Female Governor herself that I will be allowed to have prisoners to visit at any time, because of my conviction. She says the Female Governor is merely waiting for this to be approved by the Prison Governor, and that this will not occur until the next day.

Darlinghurst Gaol has never hung a woman and the gaol does not have specific rules for how to do it, is what Alice means, I think. The government and the gaol do not know how to manage my hanging, now that the judge has told them to do it.

In the meantime, Alice says, I have obtained the Female Governor's permission to bring you this chair to sit upon, with her compliments.

And so I say, Thank you.

———

In the evening, I am again taken to visit Canon Rich. I am surprised when the warders take me there, as I had thought he would go home for Sunday evening. But perhaps he does not live very far from the gaol.

It would not be proper for me to ask him where he lives.

As I enter the vestry, he greets me and says he has obtained a Bible for me, which I may take back to my cell later and read. Then he asks me how my day has been.

I sit on the chair and clank my irons onto the table. The Bible is there beside my shackles.

I have not spent a happy day, sir, I say to him, for there have been no visitors for me. I have just sat in my cell and had very sad thoughts.

He sits in the chair opposite me. Sad thoughts? In what way, Mrs Collins? he says gently.

I look at him with some amazement. Has he forgotten I am condemned to hang?

I have had no conversation all day, and have just thought of the day I had yesterday, and so I am feeling very down in spirits. The words burst out of me.

The cruel way the judge spoke to me, sir. I have been thinking of it, the way he seemed pleased that the jury found me guilty after so many trials. When he sentenced me, the judge gave me no hope and said I should find myself a clergyman.

Canon Rich looks at me and nods. And I hope I am going to be able to assist you, Mrs Collins, he says.

But the judge is assuming I done it, I say.

The jury found you guilty, the chaplain says. The judge is saying that you were found guilty by the jury in your trial and because of that, the judge has given you a sentence.

But I was only found guilty at one trial, sir, and there were three other trials before where they could not agree that I done it. So perhaps they should need to find me guilty three more times over to make up for the times they did not find me guilty.

The chaplain answers slowly. I understand why you might think that, he says, but the one guilty verdict is enough.

But after he told me I was found guilty by the jury, the judge asked me if I had anything to say about the law and I told him I did not, because how could I? I am a woman and I do not know what I might say. I cannot pretend to know the law if these men, with all their learning, do not. The law is rules made by men and given out by men and judged by men. A woman has no say in the law, as I understand it.

I said nothing, sir, through all the jury trials. They never asked me the questions they asked everyone else. They never asked me if I done it.

I see the chaplain look at me intently now.

Did you have something you wanted to say, Mrs Collins?

I know what he is asking.

The Bible is sitting on the table between us.

I calm myself.

He waits.

All I am saying, sir, is that the time the judge asked me if I wanted to say anything, I said nothing.

11.

I have no visitors again on Monday.

I sit in the cell with the warder on her chair, looking at me.

I have so much time and nothing to fill it, and I think the days will drag. I want them to be long as that will give me more time upon this Earth if I am not reprieved, but I do not want to spend that time anxious, as I feel today.

Several times through the day I have opened the Bible the chaplain has given me, to try to read a few passages.

My mind wanders. I try not to think of my sentence, as I do not want to spend my days in such a sad way as I was yesterday. I think of my childhood, and I find thinking of this calms me, just as the chaplain said it might. I sit on my chair or lie upon the bed and close my eyes and imagine I am young again. I try to take comfort in the smallest details from my youth.

The chaplain has said I might go to the vestry that evening, so late in the afternoon Warder Anderson and Warder Bryce place my shackles on me and escort me there.

Once we are settled into the chairs, Canon Rich prays.

Then, when he looks up, I do not give him the opportunity

to ask me how I had spent my day. I do not give myself the chance to complain about my sentence.

I begin with the story which I have prepared.

I grew up in some lovely places, sir, I say, and my children have often heard me talk of them. My pa would call the earliest property we lived on the land of milk and honey, which is in the Bible, sir.

The chaplain nods, Indeed it is, Mrs Collins, he says.

When I think of it, I picture a place that is always green and lush, with tall trees and the fattest sheep and the best wool. I have no recollections myself, but my father would always speak of the property in this way and so I think of it in my mind as the best of farms.

We moved around to a great many large properties and we lived all over: at Scone, Kayuga, Muswellbrook and Owen's Gap. My mother would say that my father tended us as though we were sheep in need of new pasture and a move to new paddocks with the change of the season, and she would laugh – she meant it kindly.

When I was a girl, I did not know of Sydney and all its people, or the troubles my life would bring and I was happier for it.

My mother would also say my pa was a good man who was treated ill in his youth, and while she never said how he was treated ill, my father himself would sometimes speak of his troubles, but only to her, you understand. Although children may hear anything that is said between parents.

I stop here, thinking perhaps this is not the time to speak of children and what they will hear. He does not seem to notice.

And your mother? Canon Rich asks.

My mother. I think if I wanted to, perhaps I could blame her for leading me to the current circumstances in which I find myself, for she had wanted me to marry all those years ago, when

I was happy at my work. But I do not tell him this.

My mother was a kind mother, sir, and hardworking, and I think I look very much like her, though I have not seen her for many years, and I do not have a photograph.

An early memory I have of my mother is of her dancing – she was sweeping the floor, and I was sitting upon it. I believe I have told you, sir, I am one of those people who has memories from an early age, for I could have been no more than perhaps two years old. One of my sisters was sitting on the floor with me, and we watched as our mother swept, then she sang and began to dance. I remember watching the skirts swing across the floor and she kept singing and dancing. She was swinging the broom and there was the swaying of her skirts and I still think of this memory and smile.

It is a happy memory, he says.

Oh yes, I say, I have many happy memories from when I was a child. And my mother she was a happy person – strict though, never you mind – but happy with her lot in life.

By the time I came along there were already three girls and I made the fourth. Even when we were old enough to help with the housework our mother was very fair, for she would say if we all helped, it would be done quicker. She said we would be a long time grown up and we should play while we might. And I remember happy times in my childhood, which is a nice memory to have, for there are those who cannot remember anything but work from the time they were very young. I was always mindful that my own children had some time to run wild when I became a mother myself.

I pause here and I am thinking of my children and what they might be doing and if they have heard of my being found guilty, for who will have told them? Perhaps the older boys will have read it in the paper, but I do not know if it would be written in there by now. I suppose it must be. I am glad that I was not convicted of killing their father, for that would have been a terrible thing – to have your own mother found a murderess for the killing of your father.

The chaplain prompts me. You were talking of your mother, Mrs Collins, he says. Tell me more of what she was like.

Well, I say, my mother wore her hair parted in the middle, and pulled back into a bun, as was the style. She would brush it out at night and there would be a cascade of black down her back, and she would let us girls brush it for her. I used to think her hair so beautiful, for it was long and lush, and my pa would say it was her crowning glory, and it was, sir. Oh, but she had beautiful hair, although it would be grey now, for it was turning so when I last saw her some years past. I wear a similar pulled-back style since I have been in this place, and I tuck it firmly under the bonnet, for to have my hair out will encourage all the vermin to be welcome, and they already feel welcome enough. And here, there is no way to remove them. I would treat my own children with kerosene and it always made me think of home, on account of the smell, for my parents had the legs of their bed dipped in kerosene.

Canon Rich looks puzzled.

Bed legs dipped in kerosene, he says.

To stop the ants, I say.

He nods, but I do not think he understands; perhaps he has never lived in the bush.

My mother had a fear of snakes, I say, and we always kept a snarling dog for protection from them. The dog did not have to be very big, just able to grab the snake behind the neck and shake it dead, which was frightening to watch. She preferred a dog with yellow eyes, for she said they were the best with snakes. And, you know, I have never liked dogs because of those we had when I was growing up because as a child I saw our dogs kill things. And even when I had a home of my own and the butcher shops, and there would have been plenty of meat scraps, we never kept one, as my husband Charles Andrews understood my dislike.

I suppose our houses were what you would call shepherd's huts – made of sturdy timber on the sides, and timber shingles on the roof. The floor was often dirt and there might be a piece of calico stretched across to make a bedroom for my parents. Of course, there were many huts when we were on different properties, but they were always of a similar type.

We children slept on the table in the kitchen when we were very little for, as I said, my mother had a fear of snakes and she felt the table was the safest place for us.

When we grew older, my father made us a bed of timber poles, and laced together empty wheat sacks for the swag, and we used to pull it apart and cart it about when we moved from farm to farm. But it was too soft for my liking, and with all of us in it, it would sag down until the sacks nearly touched the floor. Whoever was in the middle would be rolled in on by the others and there we would sleep, like rats in among the wool. Although our mother said we looked sweet, curled up together like kittens, I hated that bed, and missed the hardness of the table. And I used to think if a snake or rat got into the swag, there would be a terrible tumble of us all as we tried to get out. I still like a good hard bed now, sir, which is just as well for the beds in gaol have very little straw and would not suit someone used to a soft bed.

My father was a good worker and the big farms always hired him as a shepherd or a labourer. He would sometimes say that coming to Australia might have been a good thing, for he might have lost his work if he had stayed in England, on account of the machines they invented.

He said that in Australia a man could breathe clean air and eat meat every day.

And what was your father like, Mrs Collins? the chaplain asks.

He was a strong man, or so he always seemed to me, even though he was quite small. He liked to play cricket and he played even as he grew old. I suppose I would describe him as wiry. He had a scar on his forehead, although I never did ask him how he came to have it, sir. He still had a great many of his teeth, which is a blessing as one gets older. He had spent a good deal of time outdoors and so his skin was freckled and it was tough, like a piece of leather. He was not a learned man, sir, in that he had not much of his learning from books, but he knew a good deal about sheep and horses and the weather and the stars, as he spent so much time with these. He would say that there were many more stars to be seen from Australia than from England. He was able to turn his hand to most things, and so was valued on any farm. And once I heard a farm manager say that no one could raise a lamb like Henry Hall, for my father had a certain way with the sheep.

I do not tell Canon Rich that my father, God rest his soul, had no choice in coming to this country. As children, we were told never to speak of it, but it made no difference, for my father would speak of it soon enough himself when he was feeling low. That was how we heard in the first place, for he would say to my mother that he had been sent out for a crime that were not worth two bob and he had sat on the hulks and his leg had near rotted off and it were only maggots that saved him. Maggots, he would cry. And my mother would speak to him in her quietest voice. There, there, she would say and then he might weep for his mother, for they had argued when he last saw her and he had never a word from her since he came to Australia.

But I say no more to the chaplain, for I am thinking of my pa, and how he had quarrelled with his own mother and then been sent to the other side of the world and never spoken to her again and could not make amends.

Canon Rich waits for me to continue.

When I do not, he asks me a question, so as to prompt me.

You lived on a few different farms, Mrs Collins?

I rouse my thoughts.

The places we lived on were all big places, I say, such as often had their own school and might have a small station shop and even had their own church building on account of them being too far away from any town. We would go on Sundays to church and then on some Sunday afternoons there might be a cricket game in the paddock.

In the summer there would be tomatoes, as they grew wild under the shearing sheds, no matter which property you were at, and my sisters and I would go up under the shed and collect them by the bucket, for tomatoes love the sheep manure.

Often the house we lived in was wattle and daub. You would not know the house style perhaps, sir, as it is more common in the country areas, but it is built with poles of timber – young saplings which are easily cut – filled in between with pieces of mud and grass. Lovely and cool the houses were, and many are the times I have thought upon the terrace houses they like here in Sydney and how the bricks hold in the heat when the summer comes. Then, of course, wattle and daub are no help with the cold.

And I suppose life was hard for my parents, Pa with his sheep and farm duties and my mother with all the little ones, because when the children come along it is the mother who gets the most work what with all the washing and feeding. But they seemed happy.

My mother had mostly daughters, so that was a great help to her, but I have had mainly sons. My darling little May is my only daughter and I suppose has always been extra precious to me because of this, though a mother loves all her children the same, sir. Although, when my May was born I felt it was as though I was getting another chance at my own life, through her, which I think is what every mother might feel for her daughter.

I look back now and I think my childhood was too short, but I suppose it was the length of all childhoods.

Do you have any photographs of yourself as a child, Mrs Collins? he asks.

Oh no, sir, I say. I do not. The only one I have is the one which is in my head and I do not know how someone else would ever see that. Photographs were not much taken when I was a girl.

But you only need look to my May, for although her hair is fairer, she is the image of me as a child.

The very image.

12.

Whenever we moved to a new property, we would become friends with all the children at the new place, whether they were the children of the workers or the owners, as most children know no differences, sir; they only learn that as they get older. And we would play together in the afternoons, and go swimming in the dams when there was water, or riding horses, or hunting for birds' eggs and cicadas. And on one station I was particular friends with Harry, for we were of a same age.

Whenever my father was working back on that station, which he did several times, I would look forward to seeing my friend.

We came back to that property one season when I was about fourteen. I had much of the housework to do for I was one of the older girls and there were many of us children by then. Harry was the son of the owner, and so he had less responsibility, but when I had finished my chores, we would go fishing or walk through the bush, or ride upon his horse, Blackie, who was not really a horse, but a large pony, with a sleek coat and a sweet nature.

Harry said that when he grew older, he would get himself a large chestnut stallion, for he thought he should look very well mounted on a fine big horse and that when he did so, I might have Blackie. He said I looked well upon Blackie, for the horse and my hair were the same colour.

In the June holidays of that year, Harry and I spent a great deal of time together before Harry went back to boarding school in Parramatta, as was only right for a young man of his station.

The months dragged while Harry was away, for we had become particular friends. I seemed to be doing a great many chores to help my mother as, of course, with all the little ones there seemed to be always more chores to do. Harry had said I might ride Blackie while he was away at school, but I did not, although I used to go and pat him in the paddock.

When Harry arrived home at the beginning of the Christmas holidays, he found me down at the creek and he came and sat beside me. I had known he would be coming home and so I had brushed out my hair and tied a strip of linen into it, fancying this to be a piece of ribbon. I had taken the strip off a length of my younger sister's dress, and my mother had scolded me for it later, but it was the only thing nearing finery that I had.

We talked for a while and then Harry said he had a present for me and pulled a package from the pocket of his trousers. It was wrapped in brown paper, tied with string and slightly flattened from being in his pocket, and when he gave it to me it was warm in my hands and I blushed. He leant over and said to me that it was a trifling gift, as I imagine he was thinking I was embarrassed at his gesture.

But I was blushing because in the short time he had been away at school, Harry had changed and his voice had become deep and he had hair upon his face, although it was just the fluffy sort that young men get before they begin to shave properly and they are hardly men at all, but I did not know that then. And I thought how handsome he was and I think it was the first time I had ever thought of anyone as handsome, well, in that way.

I was innocent enough as to the ways of men and women, if you understand my meaning, but something about sitting beside him and holding this present warm from his pocket made me uncomfortable and comfortable at the same time.

When I unwrapped the brown paper there was a piece of perfumed soap and a cream piece of tissue with something folded inside it.

I held the soap to my nose and breathed in the smell. It was like flowers, like jonquils. I have never forgotten the smell of that soap, and of course such things might not mean much to one who is accustomed to finery, but for me I felt I was holding the smell of Heaven in my hands.

Inside the cream tissue was a piece of hair ribbon which Harry had bought for me in Parramatta. It was blue, the colour of the sky on a summer's day, with tiny bluebirds patterned along, and I thought it the most beautiful thing I had ever seen.

He said he had bought it for me to wear in my hair.

These are the things a young lady uses, he said, and I looked at him and then it was his turn to blush.

Those few months had changed us both.

The Botany Murder Case
Life and History of Louisa Collins

With good looks, attractive presence, and winning ways, she was no sooner in her 'teens' than she developed all the qualities of a country coquette, and earned for herself the reputation of being a heartless flirt. She, consequently, had many suitors and youthful sweethearts. When of suitable age, she obtained employment at Merriwa as a domestic servant, and while in this occupation was courted by Charles Andrews, whom she subsequently married, against her own wish, but under pressure from her mother, who seemed to consider she had secured an excellent alliance for her daughter ...

Evening News[10]

13.

When I first went to work in Merriwa I thought as I was moving to a very big place. Not that I would think that now, sir, not now that I have seen Sydney. Merriwa is not as grand as Sydney, for it has only a dozen streets and no trams or modern conveniences. But to a young girl who had grown up in various small shepherd's huts, when I went to live in Merriwa, well, at the time, I thought it a big town.

I worked as a domestic for the Merriwa solicitor and his wife, and I was very happy there.

At the time it came about I thought myself most fortunate to have been recommended, for it was Harry's mother who obtained me the position in Merriwa, and this was not long after Harry came home from boarding school and brought me the pretty ribbon and the soap. I do not count it quite as lucky now that I am a grown woman, for I can see that perhaps Harry's mother did not want her son to become too familiar with me, as I was not suitable, if you take my meaning.

I was at the wash tub with my mother, and I had just placed my Sunday dress into the water and was scrubbing, when the boss's wife came up the drive in the property's buggy and stopped outside our hut.

My mother went over to the buggy and spoke with her and she told my mother that she had just come from Merriwa, where she had been visiting overnight. My mother said she must be tired from her long drive, and could she offer the boss's wife a cup of tea, and the boss's wife said no, but thank you kindly, she was not stopping on a social visit. And I remember thinking this was just as well, for we only had tin cups and I was sure the boss's wife would not want to drink tea from those.

The boss's wife said again that she had just come from Merriwa, where she had learnt that the local solicitor was looking for a maid and she had recommended me for my skills and abilities.

I was surprised because I did not know that the boss's wife was so familiar with me. She said how she seen me helping my mother on many occasions and that I was just the sort of worker the solicitor required. I could hear my mother saying, Thank you, ma'am, and, Yes, ma'am, although I held myself back near the wash tub.

Then the boss's wife called me over to the carriage and told me what she and my mother had decided.

She said I was to come up to the main house the next morning and she would furnish me with a letter of recommendation and I may go on the back of the dray into Merriwa with Mr Waldock, who was one of the workers at the property, as he would be going to Merriwa the next day. She said the dray would be ready to go promptly at 10 am.

My mother seemed to hesitate then, and said did it have to be so soon, what with my father away and Christmas nearly upon us, and the boss's wife said it was an excellent position and I should be sure to take it before another girl snapped it up, and that she herself had given her word that I would be suitable.

Then the boss's wife put her nose up, in a manner that I have now seen some people do, sir, when there is a smell in the air, or someone is saying something they shouldn't. I have seen this look directed at myself more than once and particularly of late.

My mother said then that she did not mean to appear ungrateful and that I should thank the boss's wife very particularly and so I curtseyed and said, Thank you, ma'am. And she looked me up and down as though deciding something and then she nodded and drove off.

Ma and I went back to the washing, and we were quiet at first and then my ma said it were just as well that it were washing day as I would need clean clothes for tomorrow. And I looked down at the tub, and thought how all this had happened while my Sunday dress was soaking in the wash. How quickly my life had changed, and all the while my dress had lain there among the suds, just the same.

But then I have learnt since, sir, that life has many turns, and sometimes the turns are made quickly.

That night there was much preparation and my ma fussing over starching my collar and polishing her boots, as I was to be wearing them the next day. My pa was away overnight with the flock up in the top paddock, which was some eight miles away, and so he knew nothing of my new position, and I would not get a chance to see him before I left. I had imaginings of going to the stable and asking if I might take Blackie so I could ride out to say goodbye, but I did not.

The next day, I wrapped my belongings in a bundle. I had the soap and my ribbon and a nightdress, a spare dress and not much else, so it was just a small bundle. There was not much which was mine alone, as is often the way in a big family. I carried my coat, to put on over my dress when I sat on the dray, for even though it was a warm day I wanted to keep the dust from my dress as best

I could. I wore my mother's boots and it pained me to take these from her, for she had only the one proper pair, but she told me that she would wear the old pair of Pa's which she wore when around the house, and that she would let her hem down so no one would see her feet. I said I would send her money from my wages for new boots. I said goodbye to the little ones, and kissed my mother, for she would not walk me up to the house on account of her not having let down her hem yet. We shed some tears at our parting, although she said we should not, as it was an adventure I was going on, and a wonderful opportunity, and she would be sure to see me soon. I might have shed a great deal more tears if I had known it would be so long before we would see each other again.

I was anxious about not seeing my pa, as he would come back from the sheep and I would not be there and I would have liked to say goodbye to him and have him wish me well.

My mother held me close and said that she would miss me, and we both cried some more. And I wanted to think of some special words to say in return, but I could not and so I simply said that I would miss her too. Then I wiped my face and walked up to the main house.

I have often thought upon this moment and how I would have liked to have said more, as I was leaving home, and I have thought since what my words might have been. But that is often the way, isn't it, sir, that you do not know what to say just when you want to and it is only later that the right words come.

Have you said these words to her since, Mrs Collins? the chaplain asks.

No, I have not, sir, I say. It might be a foolishness after all this time.

Perhaps you could write to your mother in the coming weeks, he says, in case there were any words you should like to say to her now.

I think of how he says *coming weeks*.

I have a shadow over me until they grant me a reprieve. I think perhaps he sees the shadow cross my face because then he very gently says, Tell me more of your position in Merriwa.

Well, after I said goodbye to my mother, I tell him, I walked up the drive to the main house and went around the back and knocked upon the kitchen door and the cook said, Hello, Louisa, and so I went in.

And I said, Hello, Mrs Maisie, for that was that particular cook's name and she did not like to be called Cookie, although some cooks do. I am come to see the boss's wife and get a reference, I said. And Mrs Maisie said the reference had been left for me to collect from the kitchen as the boss's wife had said she would have no time to see me that morning, because she was in the library.

Mrs Maisie wiped her hands on her apron, and picked up a letter from the hutch in the kitchen and gave it to me, and I placed it in my bundle, but I did not read it, for it was not a letter to me, but rather a letter about me.

Then Mrs Maisie said, So you are away from us, are you, Louisa?

And I said I was, that I was to be working as a domestic for a solicitor in Merriwa, and that the boss's wife had arranged it all for me.

Mrs Maisie said, Well, did she now. That was kind. And I did not like the way she said this, sir, for there are ways some people say things as though they do not really mean them, although you may not know why this is so when they do. But later I thought that Mrs Maisie had guessed that Harry's mother was trying to separate us, for I came to learn that the cooks are often the most knowing people of all the household. Of course, I knew none of that then, for I was only a girl, and so I simply said that I would like to say goodbye to Harry as I did not know when I might see him again. And Mrs Maisie told me Harry had been up before the dawn and ridden out to the shepherd's hut that was up the top paddock. He had gone with his father to check the work of the men, and wasn't my own father there?

I said, He is, Mrs Maisie, and I bit my lip, for I was thinking how I would not get to say goodbye to my father, and how I had just parted from my mother and now I would not get to say goodbye to Harry either. I became quite sad at the thought of this going away.

Then she said that I should sit at the kitchen table and take a piece of fruit cake and a drink of milk before my long journey. She said she did not think as the boss's wife would mind, as she would never know, for she was in the library, reading a book, and there was no denying the way Mrs Maisie said this last comment – quite unkindly, as though reading a book was a sin.

And so my last meal at the property was a piece of cake in the great house. When the time came to leave, Mrs Maisie wrapped a jar of jam and some biscuits up for me, which she said I should have to remind me of my own home and she gave me another piece of cake to take upon the dray, and one for Mr Waldock besides.

14.

Mr Waldock would go to Merriwa at least once a month to get goods for the farm and so he was familiar with the place and the road to get there, and I was very glad of it as it seemed a long way to travel.

We did not speak for much of the journey, as Mr Waldock was not a man of many words, but he gladly took the fruit cake I offered and said it were a treat, having company upon the dray, and nice company at that, and then to have fruit cake to boot. There are some men who say *nice company* and they say it in a certain way, but Mr Waldock was not one of those men. I came to know as such even better in the years ahead, for he would visit me often. The journey took several hours and I remember thinking that with each roll of the dray's wheels I was getting further from my mother and father, and so I was glad of Mr Waldock, for he was a link to them.

Merriwa is such a pretty town, with the gentle hills around it, and a nice, wide main street, although I was nervous to be in such a big place on my own. I might laugh at that today, sir, now that I find my own way all over Sydney, but then I was only a girl.

As we came in along the main street, Mr Waldock said, Now you be careful, young Louisa, and mind yourself here. I will try to visit you whenever I come in, at least for a time. And I thought these kind words, and very nice of him that he wanted to see me do well.

Then Mr Waldock stopped the dray outside a large house of two storeys, with a wrought-iron balustrade and small windows in the roof. There was a garden which was full of rose bushes, and each of them covered in blooms. So there was pink and yellow and red roses all along the front of the fence. The house was not the same sort as the boss's house back at the property and it looked very grand to me.

Of course, there are many houses of this type in Sydney, sir, and they are all lined up along Elizabeth Street and George Street and there are so many that you would barely notice one above the others. They are all owned by doctors and solicitors, being as they are the ones who make all the money in the world. But in a small town, a large house such as this makes quite an impression.

Mr Waldock came to the side of the dray and helped me down, and lifted down my bundles. He said he would call at the house around the same time on Thursday next, and that he would take a letter for my mother and that I should be sure to write. And I said I would look out for him, but that I would be grateful if he would call to the back of the house as I would leave the letter there with the cook, in case I was unable to see him because of my duties. He said he would and then he climbed back up on the dray and went further up the road to the store for his errands. I stood on the path and watched him put the brake on the dray and get his knotted string out of his pocket and walk into the store.

Well, I stood for a moment and looked at the house, and I

think I did give myself a pinch for courage, for it was a grand affair, as I said. And then the pinch worked and I went through the gate and to the back of the house, to the kitchen. I took off my coat, and was glad of this, for it was a warm day, and I shook off the dust from my dress as best I could. Then I wiped my mother's boots on the mat and knocked upon the door.

A lady, who I took to be the cook on account of it being a kitchen and her wearing an apron, came to the flyscreen and looked at me up and down.

I said, Good morning, ma'am, my name is Louisa, Louisa Hall, and she said she was Mrs Roberts, the cook, and I could be calling her Cook and there should be no ma'aming about it, and I was to call my employers the Master and the Missus.

Well there, it's about time and you're here, she said, which I took as a way of welcome, for most cooks like to rule their kitchen and they often speak in this manner to give you the footing you need to start with. She said the Missus was wanting to see me.

The other girl's been gone and I'm run off me feet with all the work, she said, and I'm a cook and I shouldn't have to be clearing out slops and washing the underthings. She said Mrs Rainer came weekly and did the heavy laundry, but there were always some things which wouldn't wait for the week, and she wouldn't have Mrs Rainer do the Missus's intimates.

I learnt from that first day that Cook liked to talk but had no need that I should give her too many answers, and that if I nodded occasionally she would interpret that as an agreeance with whatever she was saying. I think it must be a way with cooks – they spend so long with puddings and flour and eggs, and other things which don't answer back, that they like to have their voice heard and talk constantly so that even if the bread could talk it wouldn't get a word in.

When I was living at the solicitor's I would hear Cook out in the morning, feeding the fowls, for even though that was the gardener's job she always liked to do this herself, and get the eggs, and she would be saying something to the hens. Now there, my little ducks, there's some nice nibbles for you, lay me some eggs for the 'morrow, I need to make me a cake. And the hens would cluck around her, and she would talk away and it was as though they would answer her.

On that first afternoon, I left my things in the kitchen and carefully retrieved my reference, and followed Cook into the hallway of the house. She motioned for me to wait while she went into the parlour and spoke to the Missus. Through the doorway, I could see the Missus sitting in a beautiful chair. Burgundy, I later learnt the colour was called. The parlour had the doors open onto the verandah, and the lace curtains were blowing gently as there was a slight breeze that afternoon. A table stood beside the chair and there was a large silver teapot, a milk jug and a sugar bowl and I came to know them well enough, sir, for it was one of my jobs to polish them.

She was sipping tea, the Missus, all dressed in black, her hair bundled loose on her head, which gave her a soft look. She was reading from a book, and looked calm and peaceful and there was the light and the lace curtains behind her, and I remember thinking that this was what Heaven was like: calm and gentle.

She looked like an angel, although one dressed in black, mind.

I am thinking of this picture in my head and Canon Rich asks me if I am thinking of Heaven.

No, sir, I say. I was not thinking of Heaven.

I was thinking of the Missus and how you can be wrong about a person, for she looked so happy and peaceful, but it was the sadness which made her like that. Or the laudanum, but I did not know about that then.

Cook beckoned for me to go into the room and the Missus looked up from her book, although I did not think as she was really reading it. She moved her arm and waved for me to come in and go around in front of her chair, which I did.

She smiled at me and said, My dear, how pretty you are, such beautiful dark hair.

And I said, Thank you, Missus.

You must be tired from your journey, she said. Get Mrs Roberts to take you into the kitchen and fetch you a glass of milk and something to eat. Then she will take you up to your room, for you will want to unpack your things. Mrs Roberts will see to everything for you and we will talk tomorrow, my dear. She waved her hand again as she said this and looked back down at her book and I remember thinking at the time that it was odd, to be so slow in everything. But that was her way.

So for the second time that day, I sat in a kitchen and had milk and a slice of cake, and the cake was good too. It was only after I had eaten that I realised the Missus had not asked to see my reference and so I asked if I should go back in to see her, but Cook said that I should not be bothering the Missus with such trifles, and I should just give my letter to her, so I did.

Then later, Cook took me up the stairs and showed me to my room.

The room was in under the roof and had one of the small windows that you could see from the front of the house. There was a tiny washstand with a basin and a jug upon it, and there was a bed. I asked Cook who I was to share with and she said, Bless you, child, this is your room. I have a room off the kitchen as it is kinder for my knees not to have to climb these stairs.

I smile at the recollection.

The room was a nice room, Mrs Collins?

It was beautiful, sir, I say.

He smiles back at me.

I can tell he doesn't understand. I try to explain it to him.

I had never had anything but I had to share. I never had one of my own, you see.

Ahh. He nods. Your own room.

Yes, sir, that was it.

Did you not have a large family, sir? I ask.

Not very large, no, he says.

So he would not understand my excitement.

The window was glass, which I thought was very modern, and you will laugh at me to think so, but most of our homes until then had a shutter-type window that you had to prop open if you wanted to see out. Of course, there were windows with glass up at the main houses and the church, but to have such a thing in a room which would be mine felt very grand. There was a pretty little curtain across the top of the window and it was tied back by a piece of cord that went to the side and hooked over a nail, so that I might draw the curtain at night, for that is the thing with glass windows, sir – you can see right through them, unless they are covered over.

There was a little table beside the bed and on it sat three pink roses in a glass bottle. I walked over and touched one of the petals.

The Missus asked me to put them roses there herself, Cook said. She wanted you to feel welcome. She said the Missus was too soft by half and I should not be taking advantage of her softness, for Cook herself would not put up with it. And I nodded and said that I would remember that.

The bed had a horsehair mattress and stitched sacking and on the top of the bed was a thin quilt made from material patterned with pink roses. Later, when I left, I was allowed to keep the quilt. But that was not until after I was married to Charles.

Cook told me the other room in the attic was kept locked and only the Master had the key and that was enough said about that. She said I should not be afraid of the Master for he were a gentleman and very kind with the Missus. She said that there was no other man in the house, as Bert, the gardener, slept out the back. The Missus tended the roses herself and Bert did the yard work, and tended to the privy and did the boot blackening and looked after the carriage and horses, although they were kept out of town and only fetched when needed.

You were happy there, Canon Rich says.

Oh yes, sir, I was, I say. They were very good to me. And it came so that I did not want to leave them.

From Whom:

The Sheriff.

Notifying that Louisa Collins will be executed on the 8th January next.

Read to prisoner.
                      Darlinghurst Gaol Correspondence Register[11]

15.

The Female Governor comes to my cell today and brings the Prison Governor with her.

I was reading the Bible, for it passes the time, and Alice and I were sitting in quiet conversation. She and I talk of the discussions I have with the chaplain. Often, after I have visited with him, I am in the mind to talk of my youth and Alice seems happy to hear this and I think the Female Governor permits our talking, on account of my being a condemned woman.

The Female Governor has walked into my cell many times since I was found guilty, but the Prison Governor has never been to see me here.

They have come to read me the death letter. The letter which outlines the date when the government hopes to hang me.

I still think I shall be reprieved.

My sentence shall be commuted to life in prison, for they will not execute a woman – they never have done so in this gaol. But now I have the date when the government intends to hang me if it can.

It shall be 8 January 1889.

16.

When I go to see the chaplain late this afternoon, Alice is with me. She seems to have been assigned to be with me during my waking hours, although at times there are other warders – Bryce and Anderson are regulars. Warder Bryce often comes at night and I am greeted by her harsh face when I wake. She is always asleep when I wake, and although she is no company at all, she does not snore like Flora.

I try not to disturb Bryce in the mornings, as I savour the few moments of time when I am able to keep my own company. I have not always liked the early morning, as sometimes I would wake with a thumping head from the night before. But I like them more now that I do not know for certain how many more early mornings there may be.

Canon Rich asks me about the death letter.

How do you feel this afternoon, Mrs Collins, he asks, after the letter that was read to you today?

I lower my head and wonder how he knows of this, but I suppose the Prison Governor has told him. It makes me wonder what else they have talked about.

I do not know, sir, I say.

It is a difficult time for you, Louisa, he says. To know your fate.

He has called me Louisa. I am normally Mrs Collins, but I suppose everything is different now.

Some see it as a gift, he says, to know when your time shall come and to be able to prepare yourself.

I lift my head and look at him.

I do not understand, sir.

To know the time that you will have left and to be able to prepare can be a gift, Louisa. I have seen it many times, in the sick, in the condemned.

I think of how he says *condemned*.

There can be a peace in acceptance, he says.

But I do not believe it will ever come to pass, sir. I have an appeal to go before the courts and they may overturn my conviction.

They may, he says softly. Although, they may not.

I tell him again that there have been three times when the jury could not agree that I was guilty and that I am hopeful the new judges might consider the opinion of these men against the twelve who did find me guilty.

And even if they do not overturn the conviction, I say, the government has never hung a woman at this gaol. I think they shall commute my sentence and I shall be reprieved.

Would you be happy with that? he asks.

I do not want to die. Then I think of spending all my time in this place.

I am not happy to be in this circumstance at all, sir. But I do not want to die.

Others are working to support you, he says. There are letters being written to members of parliament. I have heard there is a petition by the women of Sydney to have your execution commuted to life in prison.

I wonder if any of the women who are writing are the ones who come to visit the female prisoners; the do-gooders. I hope so, for the government will surely listen to good women such as them.

Would you like to write to anyone? he asks. Would you like to write to a member of parliament, or to the Governor perhaps? I could provide you with paper and pen so that you might write to your sister Elizabeth, or to your mother? Or to your children?

I say I do not know anyone in parliament to write to, but that I would like to write to my mother, and I would like to write to the children, as I have not seen the littlest ones, Edwin or Charles, the whole time I have been in gaol.

His face looks sad, and I think mine must too. He brings me paper and pen and ink.

I write a letter to my mother.

The Botany Murder Case
Extracts from the Murderess's Letters

He was tall and handsome, he was good, loving, attentive, sober, honest, respectable, fond of children, and very kind to my four little children. The love he had for his own firstborn infant was beyond all I could describe …

This man was everything a woman could wish to have. He was the apple of my eye. His voice was music to my ear. He was all I wanted in this life.

If I was between him and death, do you think I would let him go?

Oh, no fear.

Evening News[12]

17.

When I visit the chaplain the next day, we begin our talk by a discussion of how I have been sleeping, and whether I am well, which is what people talk about when they have nothing to say, or when they really want to speak of other things.

Then he turns to my story, and asks me to tell him more of my time in Merriwa.

I had no training to be a servant, sir, I say, and for the first few weeks I was lost as to what I should do to care for a grand house. I was the maid of all jobs. I cleaned the house and polished the silver and did the sweeping and the light washing of the underthings, although Mrs Rainer continued to come for the heavy linens every Monday, regular. And she was a strong woman who could wash a full set of sheets and wring them and hang them herself. She had some sixteen children, and she always looked tired, sir, but then, well, you would, wouldn't you?

Cook was kind to me in my new position. She was more of a mistress than a cook, and she did as she said she would and helped me to learn, for she liked to come and tell me what to do and how to do it and when I should be doing it. Still, she said it all most politely and it gave me some satisfaction to have her say I had done a good job, or to give me an extra scone at morning tea for my good work. She supervised everything, really. She would make sure Bert cleaned the boots properly, and help me mix the treacle and beer for him to do this. We always mixed it together in the kitchen, with Bert helping, as once the beer was open it would be a shame to waste it. They would each have a small glass and I would be sure to help myself to a spoonful of the treacle, for I did not drink beer then, and we all got on very well.

Cook herself would set the table for the meals, and I was grateful for her help, for I had no idea how to set a proper table.

It was a terribly dusty house being as it was right on the road with only the roses to stop the dust. You see, the road was not cobbled at all, though Merriwa was a busy town, and when the roads were dry you could be sure there would be a wind to blow the dust right through the house. No matter how many times you dusted, there would still be a fine layer to show up on everything. Big houses need a lot of cleaning and dusting and window washing. And even though there are not so many people who might live in a bigger house as live in a smaller house, and you would think that would mean fewer people to make a mess, the bigger ones nearly always have more things about that need dusting.

I soon learnt that the house had a routine which the Missus would always follow. In the morning she would tend the roses, and pick the blooms and prune the bushes, with Bert at her side to help her. Sometimes she would just sit among the roses and look at them, or if it was raining, she would sit on the verandah and look at them. I would do my dusting and cleaning inside while the Missus was out in the garden, and I would wear a white apron over my dress when I did my work, which looked very proper.

Then the Missus would come in for a cup of tea and wait for the Master to come home for dinner, and Bert and I would go down the road to the Church of England graveyard and I would clean a headstone which belonged to the Missus's baby. The headstone was a large one, taller than I was, with a weeping angel at the top and the angel needed cleaning every day as the birds liked to sit upon the wings and watch the snakes. And there was an urn and the Missus would place fresh roses in it each day. It had all these grooves and curves in the stone, that urn did. Roman-inspired, the Missus said it was, but those grooves did ever hold the dust.

Bert would carry a chair for the Missus to sit on and he would put the chair beside the grave and then walk back to the house. I was to wait for the Missus and the Master to walk to the graveyard and she would be carrying a bunch of roses, and she was so particular that there had to be roses upon the grave, fresh roses every day, which was very hard when it came pruning time or they were out of season.

I used to think, as I watched the Master and Missus walk down the street, that they looked like a bride and groom, except she was all in black and they both looked so sad.

The Master would pause for a few minutes and then help her to sit on the chair that Bert had brought and then he would go back to his office for the afternoon. I think he was glad to go, for it was a sad sight to see this woman sit and stare at a headstone.

After the Master had gone, the Missus would bid me to take the roses from the previous day off the grave and she would let me spread those roses on other graves nearby, even those that might not have a headstone, and clear away any I had spread the day before. I took to liking this placing roses on other graves, and it gave me something to do when the Missus sat deep in her thoughts.

The Missus could sometimes spend hours sitting on the chair, just holding her parasol and staring at the grave. Then she might suddenly stand and walk home, without any word, and I was to walk behind her, and find Bert and ask him to retrieve the chair. Cook would make the Missus a cup of tea, and the Missus would sit in the parlour with her book. I soon learnt she never read very much of the book, just sat with it upon her lap. So the day would pass without the Missus really doing anything with it, which was a shame.

There were times when the Missus did not tend her roses, and on those days the doctor would come and see her in her bedroom, and Cook or the Master would go in with him, so it was not improper.

And Cook told me about the Missus's baby and said she was so sad when her baby died that she had not wanted to give it over – had not wanted the baby to be buried, she meant – and that the doctor had to come and give her something so that they could take the baby from her, for she did not want to be parted from her child, and it was all very sad.

I did not know that type of grief then, sir, but I have since had this sadness myself and now I do understand how the Missus felt. It is such that you do not want to go on living, and you care for nothing but your own sorrow.

Cook said the Missus's baby had only lived for about six months, and that it was such a tiny thing when it was born that it had mewed like a kitten when it cried because its lungs were not very strong, but that it had the sweetest little face and the most beautiful brown eyes, which was very unusual for a baby. And the Missus had said her baby would grow into a great beauty.

The baby's lips were always blue, she said, as though it were cold, and when the doctor had looked at the little baby when she was first born, he had told the Missus she must prepare herself that the child would not live long. He said there was something wrong with her heart.

The Missus said the doctor was mistaken and there would be a cure for whatever the illness was and that doctors were often wrong and what would they know, as she was the child's mother and knew better than anyone. All the same, the Missus had bought a great many toys and dresses, and material and ribbons, as though she was trying to hurry the child into growing up, but it had made no difference.

One morning, the baby didn't wake and the Missus had taken the shock badly and been in mourning ever since.

That had been some six years previous, and the Missus had not been able to have another baby since, even though there had been two who had been started, but never been along to the finish.

After the second time, the Master had taken all the baby things and locked them in the room up in the attic, the one which was beside my room, and to which only he had the key, as he had not wanted baby things around the Missus in the hope that her not seeing baby things might shake her from her sadness.

It didn't.

Sometimes, after the Missus had been sitting at the graveside, she would go into the church and kneel and pray. And I would sit in the back of the church and wait for her, and sometimes she would be a long time. Or it seemed a long time to me as I would be wanting to go home to have my own dinner, which I did not take until after we had been to the cemetery. One time, she had been in the church for so long that I grew worried and went home to get Cook, who sent Bert for the Master, and the doctor was called and the Missus took to her bed for days.

So it was a grand home, sir, but it was a sad and sorry place as well.

I would not want to give the impression that my time at Merriwa was unhappy or that the Missus was unkind, sir. She was very kind to me.

But the Missus had become like this because she was allowed to dwell upon her sadness for so long. Sometimes folk who suffer a tragedy can pick themselves up and dust themselves off and keep going on through life, and it is often the poorer ones who do this because they don't have the luxury to stop and mourn or to sit by a grave and spend the day weeping and saying nothing. It is just as well too, for many a woman has lost a child and if they all stopped and mourned over it, no meals would be cooked and no clothes would be washed.

Mourning and feeling feeble is a luxury, and it is my observation that only the rich have that luxury, sir.

Look at the Queen and her husband, and him dead of the typhoid this many a long year, and she still mourns and wears her black, but then she doesn't have to get up and cook and scrub floors and feed her little ones, does she?

It was the same for the Missus. She had other people to do the living for her and she became content to be doing her mourning, and to just sit and let her life be lived by other people, until after a while she forgot what living really was, and thought sitting beside a statue all day, then reading a little, was enough.

I do not want to speak badly of Cook, but she was very comfortable to be soft with the Missus and pander to her unhappiness, and why should she not? She had a good position and had been with the Missus a long time, so the Missus was very comfortable in her ways.

Cook was like a mother to the Missus, the chaplain says.

I think on this.

No, sir, I say. A mother has to smack her children and tell them to behave and the like. Cook did none of this, and I think a good mother would have. The Master allowed the Missus to be sad and take laudanum, for that was what the doctor would give her when he came, and continue on in her grief.

It might have been kinder if they had told her to get on with living. Because then the Missus might have. Lived, I mean.

And I was very sad for her because she held on to her grief and let that become her life, which is not much of a life at all.

I have had my own tragedy in life, sir, and I find myself in a sorry state now, but I need to pick myself up and move on. Though I might keep on mourning for myself and what might be coming for me in January, I need to go about in the world pretending that I am not, for the world will not mourn with me. It is not that I am hard-hearted, sir, but just that I am practical.

I need to continue to have hope that I will be reprieved from my troubles, or I might begin to feel feeble myself.

18.

When I next visit the chaplain, he asks me if I have been reading my Bible.

I say that I have. That I sit in the mornings and read through some passages after I have taken breakfast.

He says he is pleased and he hopes I am finding some comfort. Then he asks me if I have been thinking any more of Merriwa. And did I ever go back to the property where my parents lived. I say that I did not, although I thought about going home, because even though I enjoyed my work, and my new life, I did miss my parents and my brother and sisters. But Mr Waldock was true to his word and on that very next Thursday he called to collect a letter for my mother.

It was only a letter on that occasion for I had not yet been paid, but I made sure I sent my wages when I had them, and the first month I sent my mother every penny, as I wanted her to have money for new boots. After that time, I kept some of the wages for myself, although when I had a large family of my own, I did look back and wish I had sent her more of my wages because I know how hard it may be to have so many mouths to feed.

And my mother came in with Mr Waldock to visit on a few occasions, when he ran his errands, although it was several months between when I left and when I saw her again, and there had been Christmas besides.

She only came to Merriwa twice that first year I was there, and she said the house looked very well, although she only saw it from the street, of course, sir. I did not take her inside, you understand. And when she visited she brought my little brother and sisters with her, and I bought some treats at the shop and we walked up to sit near the church and she told me of all the news from the property and my father, for he could not be spared from his work.

The Missus let me off on those afternoons, for it was only a couple of times, although that was still a nice kindness on her part.

I never saw Harry again, although I wrote to him, but he did not write back. Perhaps he did not receive my letters – I have always thought that this might have been the case – but it did make me sad to lose my childhood friend.

One day I did think that I saw Blackie tied up in Merriwa, but by then I was a married woman and so perhaps it would not have been proper for me to seek Harry out, and maybe it was not Blackie at all.

I kept the ribbon for many years, as the bluebirds were so pretty.

And so time went on at Merriwa and I would send a letter with Mr Waldock each month. I would tell my mother of the beautiful house and all the details of the fine silver and the curtains and the roses and the velvet chair where the Missus sat in the afternoons, thinking that my mother might like to hear of these pretty things.

And over time, Cook took a liking to Mr Waldock as he often called for letters and he was very respectful of her cooking.

I found I settled into the routine of the house and was happy to be there.

When the Missus was having a good day, she would spend only a little time at the graveside, and then when she came home, she would sometimes ask me to go and sit in the parlour with her and I would polish the silver and she would watch me and ask me to tell her stories about my growing up on the different properties. On occasion she had the thought she would like to press some flowers and so I would sit beside her at the table and we would pull the petals and place them in the sand and smooth the paper and make a picture, and put the petals this way and that. Oh Louisa, she would say, which is your favourite? And so it was that she found something to do with her time, sir, and I think it was good for her.

Later, when the Master came home, well, sometimes, he would admire her handiwork and say how beautiful the flower page was, and she might say, Louisa chose the ribbon, and then he would look to me and give me a little smile. Once or twice he said, Thank you, Louisa, you have made a fine choice, and I knew he was really thanking me for keeping the Missus from being sad.

Then the Missus said she would allow me to make a picture of my own and I said that I would be too afraid to paste anything down, for fear of making a mistake.

Now I remember when I said this the Missus gave a small laugh, and I jumped at the noise, for I had been with her for quite some months by that time and I had never heard her laugh.

The Missus was kind to me in other ways too. She gave me some patterned material for a new dress, saying she had it sitting in the cupboard and it was brightly coloured and she would not ever wear such a colour again, but that it would suit my eyes. And she arranged for Mrs Rainer to sew me a dress, and a white one besides, and she paid for these herself.

And sometimes the Missus said I might take three roses from the garden to have beside my bed.

I suppose I became something of a daughter for the Missus, sir, or so I thought at the time.

And another time, when I had been with them for well over two years, the Missus and the Master had a photographer come to the house, which was a very big thing then, sir, as photographers did not often travel out of the big cities. And I do not know if they do now even. But this one came to Merriwa. He took some photographs of the front of the house with the Missus and the Master sitting in the cane chairs on the verandah. The Missus said she wanted another photograph, one with Cook, Bert and me standing in the back, behind their chairs. We had to stay very still for the camera, but it was a nice photograph, and the first one I had ever had taken, and the Missus bought one of the photographs for each of us and said that I could send mine home for my mother so that she may have a remembrance of me.

She also bought one for herself, and placed hers upon the chiffonier in the parlour, and there I sat inside a silver frame, gazing out on all the finery of the house. And I did use to think it odd to dust myself each day, but I used to take up the photograph and look at the picture and marvel at it.

I sometimes wonder where that photograph is now, and if I still sit on a sideboard and look out at a parlour and if someone dusts me.

My mother did not like her photograph, sir, although she did not tell me this until some time after.

We went to church every Sunday and Bert and I would sit in the rows at the back of the church, and the Missus, the Master and Cook would sit up the front. Cook said she would sit with the Missus in case the Missus had one of her fainting spells, although I never saw the Missus have one of these myself.

It was outside church that I first spoke at length with Charles Andrews. I had been working for the Missus for a good few years by that time. The white dress had grown short on me and showed some of my boot, but not in an improper way, and I wore my hair down and tied loosely with a white ribbon, and on Sundays I wore a rose in my hat. I thought myself very smart.

On that day the Missus was all in black, but wore a pink rose upon her dress. I think the Master was pleased to see some colour about her as he told her how beautiful she looked, in my hearing, which is not something men do, as a rule.

I was excited that day as there was to be a cricket match in town and there would be some folk there who had travelled a great distance, and there was to be cake and sweets and it would be a fine afternoon. I was in hope of seeing my parents. On that particular morning, Bert was excused from church as he was setting up a marquee for the cricket, and so when we left church the Master and Missus had paused only briefly at the angel above their baby's grave.

Cook had hurried off to attend to her baking and I was standing outside the church, waiting to leave with the Master and Missus. Mr Andrews came up and stood beside me.

Good morning, Miss Louisa, he said. I said good morning to him, for I knew him to be Mr Andrews, the butcher, as I had been to his shop and made his acquaintance there, and I regularly saw him in church, although we had not spoken more than a good morning to each other. He held his hat in his hands and smiled at me.

Are you attending the cricket this afternoon? he asked and I said I was. He said, Then perhaps you may watch me bat, for I will be playing for the Merriwa team.

Just then I noticed the Missus and Master commencing their

walk home, and I excused myself and wished him well with his batting.

The afternoon was busy with preparations for the cricket match and Cook fussing over her baking. We went down to the oval and Bert had set up the marquee so there would be shade and protection from the birds, because they do mess so, sir, if you sit under a tree in the country.

It was a large marquee and all the ladies were to sit under it and watch the game on the chairs which he had placed there; some of them were the chairs from the Missus's kitchen and the dining chairs were there as well.

I was to keep the tea and cake up to the ladies, and to make sure they could enjoy watching the men run around. I was wearing a little apron over my white dress and a white cap on my head, and I had tied the cap on with ribbon and arranged a flower just so against my dark hair.

My father was to play cricket for the other team and so I was looking out for my mother and father, and for Mr Waldock upon the dray, and presently they came.

Now, I suppose my mother was tired from her journey for she did not seem as pleased to see me as I had hoped. She was busy with her little ones and immediately gave me my little brother to hold while she dealt with one of my sisters. He was a bonny thing, noisy and bouncy and happy to see me. But he was quite dusty from the journey and had very grubby fingers and so when he jumped on me I told him not to and held him a little distance from me lest he soil my dress.

My mother was cross and told me I was his sister and she did not matter how high and mighty I was, I should care for my brother. Or perhaps I was more interested in my new family, given that I had my photograph taken with them and they had so many fine things?

I tried to explain that I meant no offence, but that I needed to keep clean on account of working that afternoon serving tea, and she said that my employer should not be making me work on a Sunday, and we quarrelled. And, well, the moment was spoilt.

I stop talking to the chaplain here, because I am thinking back to that day, and it is as fresh in my mind as though it was yesterday, because my mother was very rarely cross, and because I had not seen her for some months.

She was probably just tired from the journey to town, Mrs Collins, the chaplain says, and he pats my hand as he speaks. What happened then?

Well, I went over to the tent, but I was sad that I had disappointed my mother. I had not seen her for some time and I had missed her and our reunion was not the one I had dreamt of. But as I served the tea, I thought how my boasting in letters and sending the photograph may have hurt my mother. Later, we made amends, but I found little joy in the day after that.

I watched the cricket without much interest, although my father batted well and scored some thirty runs, and Charles Andrews batted best for the Merriwa side. So when I later saw these two men chatting together, I assumed they were talking of cricket.

The letter from my mother came with Mr Waldock when he next visited.

I did not normally open my letters at the kitchen table, preferring to keep them and read them at night in my room. But I did read this one at the table and Mr Waldock, who was by now quite at home in Cook's kitchen, was enjoying a cup of tea and some of her baking when I opened the letter.

My mother wrote to tell me that my father had given Mr Charles Andrews permission that I should marry him.

19.

I gave a little gasp as I read the letter and Cook asked what was the matter. When I told her, she asked if she might read the letter for herself as I surely had it wrong.

I showed her, in the hope that I had made a mistake.

I had not.

My mother said Mr Andrews had spoken to her and my father and it had been arranged. She said he was a good catch and it was an opportunity for me to have a business and a fine husband.

I did not know Mr Andrews hardly at all, apart from to say hello at church or in his shop. And I did not think of him as a possible husband so I did not understand these arrangements. I had not even thought of marriage, although I had begun to notice some of the young men in town, as by that time I was of an age to do so, and I suppose it was only natural.

I could not marry without my parents' consent until I was twenty-one, and they were giving their consent to this marriage.

Cook said I should write to my parents and tell them I was unhappy with their plan for me, on account that I did not know

Mr Andrews, apart from speaking to him once at church and purchasing sides of beef from him. I wanted to mention that he was an old man, but Cook thought this was not wise as a man in his thirties was not old and it might go in his favour, for he was an established businessman and not a wild, young boy.

Mr Waldock said he would deliver the letter that very day and I trusted him to do so as he knew all of my troubles, having been sitting in the kitchen when I opened my mail.

He said he would come to Merriwa again the next week, on the pretext of a need to purchase something at the store, for he was sure there would be something off his list that they would not have today – and he gave Cook a wink at this – and that he would be sure to tell my mother that he could carry another letter back to me.

I thanked him very much and, all working together, we very carefully worded a letter to my parents.

Cook said she was sure the letter would do the trick. We should talk no more of it and we should be sure not to tell the Missus for she would worry about losing her little Louisa and then it would not happen and all her worry would have been for naught.

It was a long week that week, sir, I do remember.

I polished the silver teapot and milk jug and sugar bowl and dusted the table and chiffonier carefully, all the while thinking this might be one of the last times I would do such a thing for surely if I was to be married I would never have these pretty things again.

I begged off going to church that Sunday, saying I was feeling poorly, and the Missus said she had noticed that I was pale and silent that week and would I like her to fetch the doctor. I said no, thank you, I hoped it would pass, and that if it did not, I would get Cook to make one of her poultices.

When Cook came back, she said she seen Mr Andrews in church but she had not spoken to him, and I hoped in my heart of hearts he might have gone off the thought of marrying me.

When Thursday next came around, I was like a cat walking upon prickles, for I checked the road every minute of the morning, waiting for Mr Waldock and his dray.

He did not come until later in the afternoon, and he brought a letter from my mother, as he said he would.

She wrote that she and my father had read the letter, and they were sorry that getting married would make me unhappy, but that my father had given his word and I would have to marry Mr Andrews. My mother wrote that I should marry Charles Andrews because he was a good man and well set up and I would not do better. I ought to remember my station and if I left myself too long, I would spoil and then no one would have me.

Which I did not understand at the time, but now take to mean that I was better to marry a man of good character and prospects than to sit upon the shelf.

I cried to Cook that I should go and ask Mr Andrews not to have me, and she said I could not do that for then it would be gossip as to why.

I could not see that I had any other choice but to obey my parents and so I made plans to marry Charles Andrews.

The Botany Murder Case
Marriage Certificate

On August 28, 1865, Louisa Hall, spinster, a domestic servant, residing at Merriwa, was married to Charles Andrews, a bachelor, following the occupation of a butcher in the same district. The marriage ceremony was performed at the Church of England, Merriwa, by the Rev. William S. Wilson. The witnesses to the ceremony are given as Wm. Munro and Lucy Munro.

Andrews was a man of exemplary character, and is described as a very hard worker. He was a sober, honest, good-hearted, simple-minded man, and earned for himself the respect and esteem of all who knew him.

Evening News[13]

20.

I wore the white dress which I had worn in the photograph and to the cricket. The dress I had loved so much previous, but loved no more after that.

I spent the morning before the wedding packing my bag in my room. I looked around at the small table beside my bed and the window with its curtain and I was sorry to be going. I left my bag on the bed as Bert would bring it later to the butcher shop, and I walked down to the kitchen with a heavy heart. Cook said the Missus wanted to see me and so I went into the parlour and the Missus said I should leave down the front steps on the occasion of my wedding. She said that she would not know what to do without me, and gave me some roses to carry and oh they were such a lovely shade of pink, and she placed three roses in my hair, which I had tied up with the ribbon that had the bluebirds on it, although I probably shouldn't have, as it was given to me by Harry.

Now, I knew those roses she gave me to carry were the bunch she'd usually put on her baby's grave and that was a grand gesture for her. And I thought it nice that I wore three pink roses in my hair. I had three pink roses beside my bed on my first day in Merriwa, and the Missus gave me these on my wedding day because she remembered that, or so I have always liked to think, sir.

I did not have my father give me away as he could not be spared from his work and my mother was planning to come, but the children were sick with bad colds, and she could not travel with them. She had sent me a letter and she said she was pleased that I was marrying Charles as he was a reliable man who would take care of me. She said she would be up to see me when I was settled in my new home and she did come to visit, and I was glad of the later visit, sir, for by then I had the opportunity to make some changes to the butcher shop and the cottage, but I will come to that directly.

I had some notion of staying longer in that lovely house and being with the Missus on account we had formed some sort of a family, as such. And I know as women are supposed to marry and have children, but I was not ready, and I wondered what life lay ahead of me. There was the Missus, lost and sad with no children, spending all her time with a grave, and there was my mother, worn down by years of work and so many children. And in many ways I do see my mother was right to want me to marry Charles in as much as he was a steady man, although I would have liked him to be a little less reliable and to have more of an appetite for fun. I did not find him very interesting on account of him being so old and there being no excitement. But then I suppose a long marriage is meant to be a long time of sameness, isn't it?

Bert was to bring down my bag and some wedding presents besides, as they had been given to Charles and me before the wedding as was the custom then, although this does not seem to be followed so much now, sir. The Missus gave me a very handsome teapot, not a silver one, of course, but a good solid cast-iron one, which you may place upon the hook above the fire. I have this teapot still and use it every day, well, up until the present, you will understand. And she gave me the quilt which had lain on my bed, with the pinks and roses that I loved so, for she said she would never be able to look upon it without thinking of me, and it should stay mine wherever I went, but it is gone now, after so much moving and all the children. And she gave me a linen handkerchief, which she had embroidered herself with the initials L. A. for Louisa Andrews. And I used that handkerchief, even after my marriage to Mr Collins, even though the initials are now wrong. The handkerchief is a good strong linen.

Cook gave me a pudding wrapped in calico, and a frying pan, and the frying pan I would never part with, for it is one of the pans which also has a lid, and may be used as a pan or a pot. When I opened it, she had written out some of her recipes and placed them inside, and I cherished these, sir, for a good cook does not easily give away her recipes.

Bert had potted up some herbs and said he would be sure to bring them with him to the shop when we were settled and help me to plant them, and he gave me a digging fork, on account of him being a gardener.

I walked out to my wedding from the home of the Master and Missus, and I went out the front door, as the Missus said I may, and she stood there on the step to wave me off. Cook walked alongside me to the church, and she had on her Sunday best and her hat, and she had pinned a rose to her collar for the occasion.

Even in that short walk, I was not happy and there were many times when I would have liked to run down the street and away from my fate. And I thought of all the times I seen the Missus and Master taking that same walk from their home after their lunch, but dressed in black, and her carrying roses for their baby's grave.

I thought my face must have looked as sad as hers did when she walked to the church.

When I got to the altar, Mr Andrews and I were facing each other and I took a proper look at the man who was to be my husband, for I had not had much to do with him until we married. Mr Andrews was much older than me, though I believe he was no more than thirty-three, which is not old when you get there, sir, but I was a young girl at the time and he seemed very old.

He had a ruddiness to his complexion from days spent in the sun. He was taller than I was, although not so very tall for a man. He had strong arms and a strong back, which he had used to good advantage with the cricket bat and in his butchering. He was wearing his Sunday suit and I own he did look very smart, handsome, I would say, and neat and tidy, with his hair brushed all smooth. But even as we stood taking our vows, there was an odour about him – a meaty smell which was not pleasant.

I came to understand that no matter how long he stood and scrubbed – and I will say this for him, he was a clean man – there was always that smell about him and I took it upon myself that it was the smell from his being a butcher. I have heard of those who work in the coal pits and they have coal in their skin until the day they die, and they say there was a man in Parramatta who coughed up great lumps of black that could have been coal right out of his chest, years after he had worked in a coal mine. Well, I thought it was like that for Charles, being a butcher, it was as though the butchering had seeped to his very bones. But I really only noticed that smell in the first few days of our marriage, because I soon began to smell that way myself.

And these are not thoughts a bride should have on her wedding day.

I had wanted to have Cook as my witness, but Mr Andrews had brought two particular friends along to be witnesses, the Munroes, and so it was them and Cook who were with us and the minister in the church.

After the service, I parted from Cook and there were tears, for we had become great friends and we both knew this would now change, no matter how we pretended it might not, and then I walked with my husband to my new home. And even though it was not far away from where I had been living, it seemed as though it was the other side of the world.

My new home would be the cottage behind the butcher shop, although I discovered on the first day that the cottage was not its own building, but was separated by just a door from where the customers bought their beef and mutton.

The shop sat on a long block of land and there was a cattle yard at the back and a section where Mr Andrews would do the killing and hanging of the beasts. His horse, King, who was only a young horse at the time, was stabled in a little shed there and Charles used King to pull the cart for his deliveries, and also later when he was a carrier. I did feel sorry for King though, as his stable faced the yard, and he would watch all the killing which went on there and smell all the blood that was in the dirt. Horses can smell so much better than we can, sir, and I could smell it bad enough.

The cottage at that time was not much more than one room, although it did have a timber floor and I was grateful for that, for I had been spoilt with the timber floors at the Missus's house and would have hated to have gone back to a dirt floor.

There was a separate kitchen out near the cattle yard, and a well with a bucket, and a privy near the slaughter area. In the cottage there was a rope bed, with a blanket for a mattress and a few stumps about, which Mr Andrews said served as chairs and tables.

Mr Andrews looked about him and said he was sorry it was not grander, but that he had been used to living on his own and would be grateful if I could give advice for improvements.

I tried to hide my disappointment, but, I admit, I was sorely sorry for where I would be living.

Mr Andrews spoke to me of his plans for the shop and as he did so, he took off his suit and hung it over a nail right there in front of me, with no heed, and went and climbed into his work overalls. He told me he needed to go into the shop and open, for he might have lost business already having closed for the morning, and he did not expect me to serve today as it was my wedding day, but I was to make myself comfortable and then I could start tomorrow.

He bent and kissed me on the cheek and then he opened the door and closed it behind him, and I heard him commence to open the shop.

I sat upon one of the stumps and I cried for the pretty house that I had lived in with the Missus, and all the precious things I had dusted and cleaned and picked up and pretended were mine.

I had just turned eighteen years old.

21.

Even though Alice has told me that I have permission and may have visitors on any day, none have come again.

I do not spend very much time out of my cell, as there is no place for a condemned woman to walk and I may not join in the exercise circle in the yard of the female cell block. I am sick of these dull blue walls.

Flora has not called out to me for the last few days, which she has been in the habit of doing, and I think perhaps she has been released.

My daily visits to the chaplain give me some time from my cell, and I enjoy his calm company.

This afternoon when I arrive at the vestry, he says he has received word that most of my children will be coming to visit me soon; that Herbert will see to it that they are brought in.

The chaplain asks if I would like to tell him about my children, and I begin to. But after only a little time, I find I am not able to speak. I lower my head and think of May giving her evidence against me.

I tell him I do not want to speak of the children.

Of course, he says. It was not very thoughtful of me, Louisa.

There it is again; he has called me Louisa.

The butcher shop, Louisa, he says. Perhaps you can tell me more of the time you spent in the butcher shop.

Louisa, my own name.

The words feel heavy in my mouth. I do not feel like talking.

So he opens the Bible and reads.

When he finishes, we sit quietly.

After a time, I say to him, Well, sir, from that first day I hated everything about the butcher shop.

Oh, how I missed my pretty little white apron, and all of the lovely things I cleaned. And now I was a shopgirl in a butcher shop and had on a heavy apron and spent my day handling meat and blood. When I went home from a day's work in the shop, I did not climb the stairs to my own room with a window that looked out over the roses; I merely walked through the door to the next room, and the smell and the filth came with me.

No matter how much water I pumped from the well I could not get the smell of meat from me and I would sit on the ground and cry at the pump and Charles would try to soothe me and say it would be all right and that I would get used to it. I told him I missed the Missus and my mother, and he said he understood my missing my mother, but I shouldn't be getting airs about myself that I was anything more to the Missus than just a servant.

Now I have never forgotten those words he said because I had always thought I was more to the Missus than just her domestic and I wanted so much to believe it, but as it turned out, he was probably right.

By the end of the third week, I told Charles that I could not go on living in the hut he called a home and it was then we had our first row.

I had said I wanted him to tidy up the shop and make a proper home out of the cottage, and he said that I should be grateful for what I had, and we both of us said some unkind words. But when we had stopped rowing he said that he had got in the way of living as a single man on his own and using stumps for chairs and bathing under the pump and he would make more effort now he was a husband.

And I said we could start by keeping the door of the butcher shop shut from our home, and we would walk around the side of the building to get into the shop each morning. I said that we needed to have some furniture, such as a decent bed and chairs and a table, and a bathtub that I might wash properly at the end of the day. And I said he needed to fix the well so that I might get the water easier and to stop the blood running there from the slaughter area. He did make an effort to please me and give me some comfort, and was willing to do so, sir, but I think it was that he did not know how to go about it. He made the lean-to kitchen quite nice. Not fancy, mind you, and we still had to keep the flour and the cool safe in our room away from the rats and possums, but he put in shelves and a proper table and we used to enjoy eating out in the kitchen. We used some timber to make a garden bed where we might grow tomatoes and had onions out the side and later, when Bert came, he helped me move the soil and we gathered the manure from the yard. He would stroll past on some Sunday afternoons to see the progress of the little garden, and he always made a point of saying what a good man Mr Andrews was.

I cleaned the butcher shop properly and scrubbed the screens, for the well was a good one and we had plenty of water. And I made some curtains out of plain calico, although I have never been known for my sewing, but they looked pretty enough. We swept and put fresh sawdust on the floor, and in that way made the place look more agreeable.

Charles put some more nails in the walls of the cottage and I hung up my dresses, the white one and the pretty print, and these added some colour to the room, and I put my quilt on the new bed.

He also put up two lengths of timber so I had some shelves and could put my shoes and things on them to keep them up off the floor. Within a few weeks the room looked very homely and even Charles said how much brighter the place looked, though he was not a man to be in the way of noticing such things.

And he built me a proper clothes line, just out beyond the kitchen, away from the slaughter area and near the herb bed that I was making, so we could hang our clothes in the sun and remove some of the smell. The herbs Bert had given me for my wedding were useful and before long I had quite a garden at the back of the kitchen, growing well as they received the blood from the slaughtering. I found if I dried our clothes upon the basil and rosemary, the smell would be more pleasant and mask some of the butchering odour, but only some, mind. I would say that when I washed our clothes there would be so much meat in the water that you could throw in an onion and call it soup, and I was only half in jest.

Later, as the garden beds became more established, Charles moved the rough stumps which he had used as seats and put them out near the vegetable garden so we could sit out on a warm evening, and the herbs would counter the smell of the cattle yards, or go some way to it. And Charles planted some orange seeds, although we did not stay long enough to see them grow into trees. It was a lovely spot to sit and made me feel as though the house were bigger than it was. When it was raining I missed that little area and I used to think we would trip over each other, we were so close in our one room.

In those early days of our marriage, Cook visited often and she sometimes brought me a tablecloth or an old towel or something from the house which she said the Missus had sent for me to have as she knew it was hard to set up a new home and this would perhaps make do until we were on our feet with something better. She took to calling me Mrs Andrews but I never did get in the habit of calling her Mrs Roberts. She did not come to the cottage itself, but came to the front of the shop when she ordered her meat.

And one time when Bert came he gave me a cutting off one of the roses for, he said, if I was to plant it out the back near the slaughter pen, it would grow well. I said I would cherish it, and that he was to be sure to tell the Missus that whenever it bloomed I would think of her.

But the Missus herself did not visit, not that I really expected her to, but I had still hoped to see her, all the same.

I planted the rose in the ground so that it got all the run-off from the pen and so it grew very well and often had roses upon it.

Everyone tried to say nice things about the cottage and Mr Andrews and told me I looked happy being married, living at the back of the butcher shop, and with my own home. And I tried to believe them.

Then Cook came one day and she said she missed me and she knew how much I did not want to be married but that I was a good girl because I had done it to obey my parents and look how well it had all turned out.

I enquired after the Missus as usual, and was she well, and Cook relayed that the Missus had replaced me with a new young girl who had come in from a large property and Cook was needing to train her as she had done me.

Well, sir, I was sad to think of someone else polishing all those pretty things in the Missus's home, and dusting my face in the silver picture frame, and that I had exchanged all that for a husband and a smelly butcher shop, even though we had made improvements.

And it was about that time that I first began to like a drink.

Case of Louisa Collins

The following petition to his Excellency the Governor in favour of the condemned prisoner Louisa Collins has been handed to us for publication:—

'To his Excellency, &c., &c., &c. The petition of the undersigned female inhabitants of Sydney and its suburbs showeth, —That Louisa Collins is now a prisoner under sentence of death in Darlinghurst Gaol for the murder of her husband, Michael Peter Collins. Your petitioners pray that mercy may be extended to the prisoner on the following grounds:— 1. That it is abhorrent to every feeling of humanity and a shock to the sentiments in this 19th century, both here and in other English speaking communities, that a woman should suffer death at the hands of a hangman, and at the hands of one of the opposite sex, so long as imprisonment can be substituted. 2. That the prisoner having been tried three times for the same offence, but practically four times, is (your petitioners are informed) contrary to the practice in the mother-country. 3. That there is no positive proof of the prisoner's guilt – it has rather been assumed upon suspicion only, supported by circumstantial evidence. 4. That the fact that three juries, consisting of 36 men of intelligence, were each in deliberation many hours and during one night, and were unable to agree as to the prisoner's guilt, your petitioners consider is strong and convincing proof that the case is not free from doubt, and your petitioners conceive to be good grounds for not inflicting the extreme penalty.

5. That innocent individuals have frequently been executed on circumstantial evidence, and your petitioners entertain a just horror at the possibility of a mistake occurring by which a punishment can be inflicted irrevocable and irremediable. 6. That in the case of two women condemned to death at West Maitland for not alone having deliberately conspired to murder, but having actually murdered by poison the younger prisoner's husband – a much more heinous case than that of Louisa Collins, and one in which their guilt was proved beyond doubt, yet these two prisoners had mercy extended to them – your petitioners can see no just ground why a similar mercy should not be extended to the prisoner Louisa Collins. 7. That no execution of a woman has taken place in New South Wales for the last 28 years; and your petitioners believe that the substitution of imprisonment would act as a greater deterrent. Your petitioners, therefore, pray that your Excellency will exercise your Royal prerogative of mercy ... which is a sacred trust solely in your Excellency's hands, and which your petitioners pray you will graciously be pleased to exercise. And your petitioners will ever pray. Sydney, December 22, 1888.'

The Sydney Morning Herald[14]

22.

There is no denying that I like a drink of beer, for who doesn't when they need some cheering, except perhaps you, sir, on account of the religion. The hotel was a lively place and had lots of noise and fun and, of course, something to drink.

Charles would go on occasion and have a few drinks of beer as he said it was good for business for a man to be seen drinking, although not to excess, and he would often pick up word of cheap cattle.

So it was that one Saturday night I went with him.

I liked the taste of the beer the first time I ever had it and, even more, I liked the warm glow of joy it gave me. Right then, I felt I was in need of some joy in my life.

Mr Andrews was quite kind to me, and we were never in want of food, what with him being the butcher, but I missed my little room in the attic and the roses and I hated the thought of someone else living there. And I hated being always surrounded by meat and smell.

So it became a regular Saturday habit with me to go to the hotel whether Charles was going or not, although I do not know that I was of the age that it was proper for a girl to go, but I went anyway and no one ever stopped me. And when Charles said he did not like me drinking, I said I worked hard in the butcher shop and I should be able to have a bit of fun, and if that came in a glass, so be it.

I told him I needed to have some excitement in my life before I grew up. I was still only a slip of a lass then, and though I was married, I was still very young.

But I did grow up very soon thereafter, because one morning when I woke I needed to run out to the privy and there I was very ill, and being from a large family I knew what it meant. And it is the same which happens with most young women when they marry.

I was unwell for some time and did not serve in the shop as the smell of raw meat turned my stomach. Although I could not escape the smell entirely, it was not so bad in the cottage as it was in the shop. Cook came to the house and brought me some ginger she had taken from her own ginger plant, for she had heard it was very good for women who felt such in my condition. She had visited the shop before, but had never been into the room behind, and though I had tried to make the best of it, I looked about me and I saw where I lived as though through her eyes: shuttered windows, one room, little furniture, clothes on nails.

I did not see my mother for all of that time, although we did exchange letters and Mr Waldock called to the shop to deliver them.

I particularly missed her, for a girl will begin to value her own mother more than ever when she knows she is to be a mother herself. For it is then we begin to realise what it was that our own mothers went through to give us life. I wrote to my mother and said a child was on the way and my mother wrote back and said she would like to come and visit, and she would do that soon because my father had taken work at a property further up the Hunter Valley and she would like to see me before they left.

When my child was born the pain came so quickly that I did not rightly know what to do, but I was lucky in my way and I will leave the description at that, sir, for it is women's business and a delicacy which should not be shared with a man, even if he is a chaplain.

My boy was bonny and healthy, and hungry. I named him Herbert. I was so happy to have him that I did not look on the cottage as small any more, for it was filled with my child. For a time, Mr Andrews would sleep out in the kitchen on a low bench we had there – the lid of the woodstack box – for he wanted me to have time with the baby, and Herbert slept in the bed with me. Charles no longer expected me to work in the shop as I had the baby to care for, and he was a good father from the very start.

My mother and father and my younger siblings all came to visit, and I was able to show them my beautiful boy, and my mother was pleased to see for herself the improvements I had made in our cottage, as I had written to her of these. She thought the shop and the cottage all very well and we spent a nice afternoon out near the herb garden. My father and Charles got along very well and my mother admired Herbert and said he was a fine boy and we spoke of babies and the new property they were moving to. And I thought I should be happy enough to be married to a hardworking husband and have a handsome baby, and a shop and a house, although a small one.

I felt very sad when my parents left.

I was standing with the baby at the front of the shop, and Charles had his arm across my shoulders, and we would have looked the perfect young family. But I was thinking of my parents and that they were leaving me at my house, and I never would again be their little Louisa, and I was not my parents' child any more, and I was not the Missus's domestic; I was now my husband's wife, and a mother.

And I would never again be just Louisa.

Or perhaps, sir, it was simply that I missed my mother.

23.

In the afternoons, I used to swaddle Herbert in a shawl and walk with him down the street. I wanted to take him to see Cook, but did not know if it would be the best thing for the Missus, and also, sir, I did not want to see the girl who had replaced me.

We arranged to have Herbert baptised in church and I stood at the altar in the white dress and held up my beautiful baby boy. Mr Andrews stood beside me and everyone clapped and said what a grand happy family we made. I nodded at the Missus and smiled at her but she did not smile back and afterwards, when everyone crowded to see the baby, the Master and the Missus seemed to head off home quickly.

Cook came to see me the next day and said that the Missus's spirits were not good and the Master had asked for me not to show off my baby to her like that again, and he sent five pounds for me to put away for Herbert for his schooling.

I said I had meant no harm, we were just proud of our baby and showed him to all at church, and Cook said she thought I would have more sense than to do this in front of the Missus, and I should have sent word that I would be taking the baby to church as I knew how the Missus might be, seeing a baby. I told Cook that I thought it was high time the Missus snapped out of her melancholy and got back among the living and, well, sir, our visit did not end happily.

But I kept the five pounds for Herbert.

Before long, another child was on the way and then my boy Ernest was born. I did not think I could love another child as my heart was so full of love for Herbert, but as a mother you find more and more love for each baby, and that has been the case for me, sir, with all of my children.

I was kept very busy, with two boys to care for. Ernest was only a little thing when he was born, although he grew well enough.

24.

Not long after Ernest was born, Charles heard of a carting business in Muswellbrook being for sale, with a larger cottage into the bargain, so he decided to purchase the business and we moved.

At the time, I was not sorry to leave Merriwa, for I did not like to see the Missus and her new girl in church and about town, and Cook and Bert did not come and visit the way they had, though we were polite enough when she came into the shop for her meat. I thought that a move to a new town might be just the thing for Charles and me, and my own parents had moved around a great deal, so I was used to it, sir.

I dug up my rose bush and put it in a tin pot, for I had seen my mother do the same with plants when we had moved from farm to farm.

In Muswellbrook, things went well for a time and we soon had another baby, my boy Reuben. Charles had plenty of work as a carrier and he and King were kept very busy. I went with him once and the children and I visited my parents for the day, as he was going to be near where they were working at the time.

But my little Ernest began to be unwell and have fevers and he threw several fits and these were terrible to see. When he was about three he caught the croup, for it were a particularly bad winter for croup and after that, well, I never thought his lungs were quite right, as in the months which followed he seemed to always have a cough or a cold. I tried the rubbing of the camphor and the soaking of his feet, but nothing would seem to bring the boy any relief.

One morning he simply did not wake. We had heard nothing during the night. We had the habit of taking our little ones into bed with us when they were unwell. He was just lying there when we woke, and for a time I thought he was asleep.

He looked so peaceful, sir.

We laid him on the kitchen table and the arrangements were made. I did not have time to get any proper mourning, although we had no money for such things either, as when you go into mourning proper, it is to be new clothes for the whole family.

He was buried at the church in Muswellbrook, in a little grave up the back. Charles and Herbert and I walked there with the minister and Charles carried the coffin. He had made the coffin from rough timber and he laid the little box in the ground. I held Herbert's hand and also carried Reuben, who was only a baby, and he wriggled and squirmed as they do at that age, him not knowing what we were about. Herbert, I think, understood, being older.

When the soil was covered over, I had a single rose off my own bush and I placed that upon the bare soil. Then we stood and looked at the piece of ground.

I did not know what I should do, without my beautiful child.

But as we stood there I thought of my little boy, down under the ground, all alone, with no mother to hold him, and I could not bear it. I said to Charles that we should dig up the box and open the lid, that I might hold Ernest one more time, and that I needed to have a lock of his hair, but Charles said it was too late. And I said it was not and I needed this as a remembrance and then he took my arm, very gentle he was, sir, and he patted my back with his other hand and said it was too late, and I began to cry, for I had not really had a good weep until that moment. It was the shock of it all, I suppose.

And then Charles took hold of Herbert and Reuben and we walked home.

I thought as my heart would break on account of losing Ernest, for it is a terrible thing to lose a child.

For a while, I suppose I became a bit like the Missus, because I visited that little patch of soil up the back of the cemetery every chance I could, although it was not every day. And I worried about that lock of hair, as I should have cut it when he was with us and I would have been able to cut it if only my husband had dug up the box when I had asked him. But of course it was too late for such a thing, even a day after.

Sometimes I would visit the grave at night as well, after I had been to the hotel, and I would sit there after having had a few drinks, and I would talk to my little Ernest. I did so want to have some sort of marker upon the grave, and I used to think of the grand statue that the Missus had for her child and I wanted something like that for mine. Charles made a simple timber cross which we placed into the ground, and it said Ernest Andrews, but I suppose that has rotted away now, as the timber markers do not last.

This was the beginning of our sad times.

After working carting for some years, Charles went back to butchering, and we had a shop and the house which came with it. The shop went well in the start and Charles said we would own it outright before too long, for he had borrowed money to buy the shop, sir, although I do not rightly know exactly how much, for he did not discuss our money with me. The house was not attached to the shop, and so it did not have quite the same smell of meat, and the slaughter yard was on the next corner, so King was able to have his stable away from the blood.

But then business dropped away and we began to lose money, so we moved to a smaller house. And then Charles cut his arm. He was slicing up an old pig and his knife slipped and slid straight up his arm, but it did not make too much of an injury and the cut was so small that it did not even need stitching and so at first he was not too worried. Being a butcher, he often had cuts from his work. But the wound got infected and before long he had great streaks of red creeping up his arm and I needed to apply potato poultices to ease the infection out, and Charles took to his bed. Oh, sir, he was very ill, and stayed abed several days.

We had a young boy, Thomas his name was, come to work in the shop while Charles was ill and Thomas gave all who would listen updates on the infection. And it was his mouth that was the undoing of us because word spread that Charles was unwell on account of an infection from a pig, and so when Charles went back into the butcher shop there were those who would not buy meat from him. There was another butcher shop and so many of our customers simply went and bought their meat there. Even though Charles had been working for years as a butcher and this was the first time he had been ill.

And then we struggled to repay the loan we had taken out. Of course it cost us more to live as we now had five children, for we had added Arthur and Frederick and May to Herbert and Reuben. The five were not counting little Ernest, sir, buried in the cemetery.

I cannot rightly recall all of the details, but Charles came to think that he would be better off working for someone else and that we should move to Sydney.

So this was what we did, because by then we had lost the business and our home. The man we owed money to was a kind enough man, even though he was rich, and he allowed me and the children to stay in our house while Charles rode to Sydney to see about work.

Charles came back saying as we should try our hand in the city, for he had been able to get work as a labourer until we could save the money to buy another shop, and he knew Sydney, sir, for he had lived there previously.

We packed our dray and hitched up King, and brought our few things with us and headed to Sydney. I wrote to my mother to say that we were leaving Muswellbrook and moving to Sydney and that I did not know the address where we would be staying, but that I would let her know just as soon as I did. It was a sad day when we drove out of town, because we'd driven into Muswellbrook with such hopes and we had begun so well.

But after our time there, nearly some ten years it was, we were leaving and leaving our dear little boy in the cemetery and owing a great deal of money, so it was not at all as we had planned. Charles did not like owing money to anyone, sir, and he worked hard to pay back all he had lost, and so my parents were right about him being a hardworking man, and though it made life hard for us to be repaying what we owed, we did try to repay it. When we left Muswellbrook I remember I was nervous to be leaving the country, for I had never been to Sydney before, although Charles had told me many stories about the city.

But had I known what was awaiting me here, sir, and that I would be locked up in this place?

Then surely, I would never have come.

25.

We did not exactly move to the middle of Sydney, for I have since learnt the size of this city and the centre is a long tram ride away from where we settled. But to someone from the country the city is all the same.

We moved about but the area we eventually settled in was called Botany Bay, although you will be no doubt aware of that, sir.

The trip to Sydney is one of the happiest memories I have of Charles, for even though we had left owing money, we both enjoyed the journey down – camping with the children on the side of the road and making a little fire at night and then sleeping on the dray under the stars. We made steady progress from Muswellbrook to Sydney as we wanted to hurry for his work, because he did not want his new boss to give the work to someone else.

I said that it would be a nice way to live, like a gypsy, travelling and sleeping by the side of the road, and he said it would at that.

This was the only time I could remember him not working, and he was a different man, sir, and not so tired.

Though it was a nice journey, it was only when we were on the road that I perhaps realised how far away Sydney was. I did not like the thought of going away from my parents, even though I did not see them as much as I would have liked. Sydney seemed to be so very far and I wondered if I might ever see them again at all.

And I never did see my father again, sir.

And now I think of how I may never see my mother.

But you may write to her, Louisa, the chaplain says. You may write as many letters as you need, now you are in this situation.

Situation, I think.

Tell me more about first coming to Sydney, Louisa, he says.

Well, sir, I say, apart from this consideration, well, I suppose I began to allow myself to be caught up in the excitement of something new. Mr Andrews told me of some of the sights which could be seen in Sydney. He told stories of the big harbour and the towering buildings and the shops and how many streets had been cobbled. He had lived in Sydney as a younger man, although much later when I learnt how the city had driven his own father to such distraction, I wondered why he should be bringing his family there. But I was a wife and so I followed my husband where he led, and, also, I did not know the details about his father at the time.

When we came to the outskirts of the city, everyone seemed to be in a hurry. We had stopped at a crossroad and two men approached the wagon and made to take hold of King by the head, on the pretext of taking us where we were wanting to go, but my Charles shooed them away, making it clear that he knew where we were headed, and they left sharply.

I marvelled at the sights to be seen. All the ladies wore fine dresses and big skirts and carried umbrellas. There seemed to be hundreds of women all over the city, all dressed smartly in black and grey and all busy walking to somewhere else.

When I first saw the great harbour, well, sir, I could not believe that such a big piece of water could be a bay and I thought it was the sea. I said to Charles that surely England must lie on the other side of all that water, and he laughed, but not unkindly. And when I think back, I am inclined to laugh myself, but you can imagine, sir, what it was like upon first seeing such a large thing.

My own father had once spoken of coming to Sydney and he said a more beautiful harbour you would never see, and no doubt he was right although I have not seen any to compare.

Charles's work was across the other side of the city and we still had a day to travel, and so we pulled over. We camped in a park on the wayside and Charles assured me that the following day's journey would not be so long and that we would be in our cottage by the next night.

I did not sleep so well when we were close to the city, for it is one thing to be sleeping under the stars in the bush, where you must only worry over snakes and bandicoots, but quite another when you are in the city and must worry over thieves, for we had little enough and I did not want it stolen.

The next day, we still seemed to go a long way, and I recall thinking there could never be a place with so many streets. But we came to the place they call Berry's Paddock and Charles took the work he had arranged. He worked for a bone dust factory, which made fertilisers, and he worked there several times over the years as the work required.

And it was while we were living there that I had my seventh child, my boy Edwin. A woman from Berry's Paddock helped me with the birth.

We did not stay in Berry's Paddock long on that occasion as Charles soon found better work.

We moved to Botany, to an area called Frog's Hollow. I

believe it is called this on account of the many frogs who live there, for they do make such a noise.

At Frog's Hollow, we had to leave the wagon and horse and walk across a small footbridge to the cottage. I left one of the older boys, although I cannot remember which one, standing with the horse, with instructions to call out if anyone was to try to steal our cart.

There were a few cottages around, a row of neat little buildings, and I learnt one of these was to be ours. Pople's Terrace the cottage row was called.

The address of our cottage was number one and we were very pleased with what we found. It was only small, just the two bedrooms, but it was well built and it had glass windows.

There was a front room, and then a bedroom off to the side, and then a back room that led to the kitchen. Behind the kitchen there was a yard which had a little washhouse and an area for the privy. Beyond that was scrub and swamp, and you could head down a little path to a type of beach area, or a swampy ground, where the children set to playing.

Charles said there would be milk deliveries, and the baker would come and bring his bread on the back of his old cart.

And the night soil man came, which we had not had before, although he was not one with whom you would socialise, sir, but someone you were always glad to see, nonetheless.

There was a hotel and a grocer, Mr Sayers, who was just up the road from the cottages, and later that day his worker came down as we settled in with our furniture and gave us a loaf of bread and a small pot of jam, saying this was with the compliments of the grocer and asking if we could return the pot when we had finished the jam.

Charles was quick to say how friendly the grocer was, and I suppose because I was tired and the baby was fussing and irritable, I said they had sent the bread and jam to ensure I bought more from their shop when I took back the pot. He said that was unkind and I snapped at him and we quarrelled some, as husbands and wives do. I thought better of my words later and so I said he had done well to find us such a comfortable home, and I would be sure to go to the grocer shop and thank them directly.

Perhaps it was our quarrel, I do not know, but I found it hard to sleep that first night in Pople's Terrace. There was the strangeness of having new people right upon your doorstep and I could hear noise coming from the various sleeping quarters in the cottage row.

Charles slept out on the dray that night, for it filled the whole of the laneway and he was feared someone might steal it. He hobbled King nearby.

Before dawn, I got up and gave Charles some tea and bread and jam, which was some of the jam from the grocer, before he went off to the fellmongers where he was to work. He was to take the dray and King with him, for he had arranged to sell them to his new boss as part of the deal for his position as we had found King hard to keep in the short time we had been in the city.

I stood and patted the old horse, for he was quite old by then, sir, and I told him that he was a good horse and had served us well and that as I may not see him for a while I would miss him. I stood for quite some time rubbing the nose of the horse, while Charles had his tea and ate his bread. I hope whoever took King treated him well, but I suspect he went to the knackers.

The children were still sleeping as Charles turned the wagon to go to his new employment and the first rays of the sun were smearing the sky. It was as though blood washed upon the black on account of the great streaks of red, not yellow as normally greets the morning, and I shivered. I remember standing in the road, watching my husband walk away our horse and dray, and I recalled the saying.

You know the one, sir?

Red sky in the morning … shepherd's sure warning.

My father was a shepherd, sir, and so I knew what that sky meant.

26.

In the first few weeks that we came to Pople's Terrace, we were a great novelty in the road, as any new family moving into a street always is. The children made friends with the children of the neighbours and the boys, particularly being of the age to do so, played cricket with the other boys, and they would be out on the road playing for most of the day. I had no concerns about them being on the road, for the trams did not come that far and no horses or carts ever came up the street as they couldn't cross the footbridge.

Now, as I have said, the cottages were close to each other, and we all shared walls and these were thin, so all of our stories were known to each other for there are no secrets in such places. If one couple is rowing, well, you can hear it all over. We all lived in each other's pockets. And so we soon knew each other's most intimate business and we were in and out of each other's houses and the children played together, but I had experience of this, from living in the country, and so I knew about gossip.

Charles settled into a routine there at Pople's Terrace and found plenty of work.

And as for me, well, by that time, I seemed to spend all my

days cooking and cleaning and tending the little ones and so in many ways it did not matter whether I was in Sydney or Merriwa or Muswellbrook. But I did find the noise of so many families all jammed in together very tiresome and so I tried to get out of the house each day, and at Frog's Hollow I would often go to walk along the track on the other side of the woolwashers and the tannery to the little swampy area, taking the children with me.

It was a marshy beach, more of a swamp I suppose, and in some parts the water was quite foul and smelly from the Botany factories. But a little further down was a small creek and there the water had just a brown tinge, I think from the tree bark, or so I was told. The children enjoyed skipping through the shallow water. There were tiny fish to chase and the children would cover themselves with the mud from under the trees and scrub it into their skin, which I would allow provided they would get the sand from the swamp and scrub their legs and arms afterwards because there is nothing such as sand to get a body clean, sir, even better than soap. And sand is free to use.

I did not romp in the water myself but on occasion, if the weather was particularly hot, I would lift the hem of my skirts and slip my bare feet into the water. It reminded me of my own childhood, and the happy times when I would swim in the dam with the other children and so it gave me great pleasure to see my own children having the same sort of fun. Although in some ways it made me sad too, sir, as at times I felt very old, thinking of being a child and now having so many children myself.

And so we settled in and made our life here in Sydney.

We had been living in Botany for nearly a year when my next baby, my David, was born. Even though he was my eighth child, he was a difficult birth. He seemed a weak baby from the first and had to be smacked several times before he would cry.

David had something like the fits that my boy Ernest once

had, although of course Ernest was older. Oh, it is a terrible thing for a mother to watch, sir.

Cruel is what it is.

My baby David died in my arms when he was but twelve days old.

He had been fitting that morning, throwing his head back and making no noise. His body then stiffened and his eyes showed their whites and he held his breath. Then he went limp, and I waited for the gasp, but it did not come.

I rolled him onto his belly and he flopped over my arm, his little head dangling forward, and I shook his body but he did not breathe.

I called out for help and one of my neighbours, Mrs Malone, came in and saw David, and saw me swing him over and shake him.

I rolled him onto his back, but he had not yet breathed again, and Mrs Malone put her mouth to his and tried to breathe life into him, for, she said later, she had heard this could be done. After a few minutes, she placed her hand on my arm and took the baby from me and wrapped him in his blanket.

Then she sat me in the chair and gave me the tiny body.

I allowed myself to cry, and I was very low, sir, as it is a terrible thing to lose a baby, and I was tired, for I had not slept much since his birth. I thought of my boy Ernest, who had died many years before when he was but a little older. And I thought of him lying in his grave, with no one to bring him roses.

Someone went and fetched Charles from work, and he came home, took the baby from me and held him in his arms.

David is buried at Rookwood cemetery, I believe, for Charles saw to those arrangements and I did not travel out on the train.

I do not think the grave is marked.

The chaplain asks if I would like to pray for David with him, and I say I do, and so he prays for all my children.

27.

The next time the chaplain and I speak, we are in my cell. He has come to visit me here and we sit upon the chairs. The warder stands in the corner.

It is not as pleasant as in the vestry, as there is no table and the slop bucket is in the corner.

But I do not need to wear my shackles, so there is that.

We talk again of my baby David.

Charles and I had been married some sixteen years when our David died. We had less money than when we first married, when my mother thought she was making such a good match for me. Two of our children had died, which puts a great strain on a marriage, sir, and we still owed money from our time in Muswellbrook. We had a large family with Herbert, Reuben, Arthur, Frederick, May and Edwin, and the older boys were eating the amount of grown men, though they were not yet earning a full wage. They would sometimes work alongside Charles if there was the opportunity, sorting and carting the green skins from the sheep – those which are stripped off the freshly slaughtered animal – but it was not regular work.

We quarrelled more. And whenever we had words, I would visit the Amos's Pier Hotel, as it was only a few doors up the road from where we lived.

You will not have seen this hotel, I think, sir?

Oh, it is nice, although not very grand, but there is an area for ladies to sit and the bar is made of one solid piece of timber with a looking glass running right along the back of the counter, so as to give more light and reflect the gaiety of the patrons. Of course, Botany also has the Sir Joseph Banks Hotel, but that is a bit further away and it is a sight to see, with a menagerie I believe, and I have heard there is even an elephant, but I never saw this animal myself.

Well, Charles begrudged me the time I passed at the hotel, and the little money I spent there, although he himself would go every Saturday evening, regular. But he was not a big drinker and for that I am grateful, as some men will be violent with too much drink in them and he was never that, was Charles, although he did argue badly with Michael Collins on just one occasion, but that was not his normal character, you understand.

I cannot rightly remember when it was, but it was after one of his Saturday night sessions that Charles took it upon himself to come back home with a gentleman in tow, who he had met that very night and who had arrived in Botany to seek work as a woolwasher. Charles walked into the house and settled this man in the back area near the kitchen. I was not pleased that Charles had brought a man I did not know into our home for the night and I told Charles so when we went into our bedroom. We argued quietly, in that hissing way that you do when you do not want others to hear, and I said to Charles the same things that I had said when we spoke on the subject previously – that I was not in favour of boarders because our cottage was not big enough and they would be extra work. He said we needed the money, and I said there would be more mouths to feed and more washing and that I would have to do all of the caring for the boarders and he said what was it that I thought he did all day while I was playing with the children.

That hurt me a great deal, sir, for it is a lot of work to care for children, and do all the washing, and cook the meals, and there is the drudgery of it – doing the same thing every day and knowing you will need to get up and do it again tomorrow.

Then Charles said we should not quarrel as our new boarder would hear and he showed me the coin which the new boarder had brought with him and said that I may have that to spend as I pleased. So I softened a little to the idea of boarders, and as it turned out our first gentleman was an easy boarder to have – always paid his rent regular and normally only ever took a cup of tea from our table, although he did have a meal with us on occasion, but that was not a regularity. He was never any trouble, and he boarded with us for some years, coming and going whenever his work brought him into Botany.

Charles said he would like to bring in other boarders, and there is no denying their coin was much needed, and so I agreed. Soon there were so many people living in the house that I felt there was always someone underfoot, if not a child then a man. The house was crowded and we were all jumbled in together. The younger boys and May slept in our room and the older boys slept on the stretchers in the front room, which was the sitting-room parlour. We would lay the stretchers out for the older children at night, and then fold them up against the wall when they were at school or at work, but it became such a chore to do this when they left for work at four in the morning that eventually we would just leave the stretchers out and the house was always untidy. But we did use one of these fold-outs for Charles when he was sick.

The men who came as boarders would sleep in the back room, near the kitchen, and there were some who worked different shifts, so they would share a bed, as it were. We made some accommodations for the number of people in the house and bought a larger table for the kitchen area and a second bath, so that on Saturdays the men might have a cold bath before they got into the warm tub, and that way they would wash off the worst of their dirt in the cold and still have some warm water left to share for the last man in. I left the organising of the men's bathing to Charles. I did not stay in the house on a Saturday after heating the water and making the preparations. All the men would be in a state of undress during their bathing, and so Saturday afternoons became an opportunity to sit at the hotel.

My own bathing arrangements would be undertaken on a Saturday morning, with Charles standing guard on the door to protect my modesty.

I was strict about the men walking to the pump and washing before they came into the yard from the back of the house, as I said I was not carting water for that many men to wash off their filth from work, as the blood and pieces of wool which came home with them might as well be slops for all the mess and smell. Oh, there is nothing like it, that sheep smell, sir. And I said that I had to cart the water for the Monday clothes wash, and that was job enough.

When we first took in boarders, there was all the gaiety of getting to know new people, and the house full of chatter and the door always opening and closing and so many stories from all the different people coming and going.

Having so many extra people in the house made for a bit of a change, and they took a great interest in the children. And on occasion, we would send one of the children along to the hotel for a jug of beer, and then we would sit and share some laughs.

But I would not like to give the impression it was easy having boarders. Some of them became like visitors who overwore their welcome and others expected me to act as their mother and pick up after them and cook all their meals even though that was not in the terms which were offered. The house was always crowded, with everyone talking, and eating, and there was always dirty washing and dirty dishes and people coming and going and heading out to work at different times. There was always someone wanting something, a child crying or wanting to be fed or with a snotty nose or filthy pants, or a man saying, Missus, if you don't mind ... and then they would be wanting a button sewed or a cup of tea or whatever their fancy was at the time, for some men who come as boarders seem to be unable to put one foot in front of the other without being told to.

Nearly all of the boarders enjoyed the noise of the children when they first arrived and called them their little pets and darling treasures and then would change their tune and be annoyed by the children and all the racket. There was always someone in a state of undress and I began to not know which way to look, for there was always a man in front of me half covered up. And there seemed to be so many extra mouths to be fed, and so much more washing to be done, and with just me to do it all.

It was about this time that I had a falling-out with one of the neighbours over some clothing which went missing. With so many people in the house, I would try to escape and take a walk with the children down to the edge of the swampy beach, and I would sit and look out over the water.

I think I have described this area to you before, sir. Even though it was swampy and somewhat smelly, although not as smelly as it has become, for there are a great many more houses and privies and such, I would take the children to the water and I would take down some of the washing, for even if it was not Monday there would always be dirty washing to be done.

The children would run and play and I would wash the clothes in the little creek, which ran out into the swamp area, as the water was slightly deeper there. It was not a real wash, mind, just a rinse to see us through, and so I could keep going with the work while the children had a play in the creek. I had a piece of rope strung up as a clothes line between two old paperbarks and I would hang the washing up. Never privates, you understand, just the outer garments and towels and the linens and the like. And I would sit and watch the children frolic as it dried. Sometimes I would leave the washing there overnight if it did not dry proper, for the neighbour, Mrs Malone, had said it was quite safe to do so. I would collect the washing when I went back the next day with the children.

On this particular occasion, the children and I went down to the swamp. I had done quite a large wash, for the weather had been poor and raining on the Monday previous and my washing had built up. I left several pieces of the wash hanging overnight and when the children and I went down the next day, it was gone. Now, I thought perhaps one of my neighbours had brought my washing in for me.

I went back up the path and stopped at the first house along, which is the house of … no, I will not say whose house it was, sir, for we had words on that occasion.

I looked along her yard and saw nothing upon the line, but just then the lady came out of the back of her house and so I asked her if she had brought my washing in from down at the bay. She said she had not, and that she knew for a fact none of the other women had either, for she had been with them that morning and they had not mentioned it.

I asked had she been discussing my washing with them for her to know that and she said she had not, but …

And there she stopped.

I said, But what, for it was obvious to me that she had intended to say more. And she said that she just meant she was sure they would have mentioned it if they had brought in my washing for my washing had been a topic they had discussed previous.

Why had they been talking of my washing? I asked her.

She told me that some in the neighbourhood had talked of how I left my washing hanging down among the trees like a gypsy and that I did not take the time to boil the copper like a proper mother should and how the clothes would never get clean by just being washed in a creek.

She said when I had asked Mrs Malone about the hanging of clothes down near the bay she was not given to understanding that I would be washing the clothes there too.

And I said some harsh words and that the women of the neighbourhood might have taken the clothes themselves, for they were such ... well, I will not repeat what was said, sir, on account of your religion, but it was not a kind name and one that is said about women of a certain type.

Then she said that no other woman in the street would have touched my washing, except that a good housewife might take it in and wash it with hot water, and clean the clothes, and she folded her arms across her chest as she said this as though daring me to say more.

I didn't.

I walked back down to the bay and sat on the ground and cried my heart out, there being no one to see me. I had had a fight with the neighbour and I had lost my washing and I never did find it, and one of the things I lost was the coloured dress. Of course, by then it was not brightly coloured and it had worn threadbare in places and been remade twice, but I did sorely miss it.

It was one of the last things I had from that other life with the Missus.

28.

I did not hang my washing at the creek again, and with so many boarders the backyard became a maze of washing lines, and it made the house seem even smaller.

On wet days, the washing would be strung around the house and it would seem that the men would be strung the same, lounging all about the parlour, with not a bit of privacy for a woman. Sometimes not even as much as a chair to sit on and call her own.

If I was feeding a baby, I had to go into the bedroom and, as there was no chair, I would sit upon the bed.

All of the boarders who were with us at this time were men that Charles had brought home, having met them at the Amos's Pier Hotel when he went for his weekly drink or having worked with them at one of the factories. They were mostly older men who were either single or had not yet brought their families to Sydney and were trying to find their feet.

They helped with the money side of things, sir, but it became very hard for us, for Charles and me, to continue on as a man and wife with me being the landlady to everyone. I found I needed to stretch the money more. There were extra candles required and more tea and milk. We did not supply meals as a rule, but I did give a breakfast of bread and jam to the men, as most of them went off to work early and I would not see a man head off to a day's work on an empty stomach. And there were occasions, when Charles had butchered a pig or such, that I would cook a roast and they would all partake, for an extra coin, of course.

Still, we were managing to repay some of our creditors from our time in Muswellbrook, for Charles did not like to be in their debt.

Charles permitted the boarders to have a few drinks, but he was most particular that they were moderate, and he would tell them when they first moved in that they would not be welcome if they took too much to the drink. He liked well enough to sit out the back, for we had a little area where we had a few stumps placed and a fireplace in the middle, not unlike the place we had made in Merriwa, and I would boil the copper on that fire to do the wash every Monday. He and the men would sit and send the children to the pub for a sixpence of beer.

We would sit just at the back of the kitchen, quite a nice area, though you could still see the privy.

I had some geraniums growing beside the privy, for my mother always liked to have a geranium growing there and would plant a cutting at each of the places we lived. She said it would make that place nicer to have a few flowers about and a geranium never took much water and of course there are those who say that a geranium will keep away the snakes.

The yard was not a big yard, but there was a fence between it and the track to the pump, and the swamp of the bay. We had some tomatoes and pumpkins growing over the fence. Pumpkins are handy additions to have, sir, when you are trying to feed a lot of hungry mouths. And roast pumpkin with a leg of mutton is very tasty. I recall one of our boarders, Mr Peters, one of our early boarders, he said he had heard that some folk would not eat pumpkin themselves and would only grow them for lanterns and to feed to the cattle but he felt they were surely missing out for the way I cooked pumpkins was a real delicacy and make no mistake.

I would have liked Cook to hear that, sir.

Beyond the fence we had two small orange trees, as Charles had planted the seeds when we first arrived at the house, even though we were only renting. The seeds had grown into strong little trees in the five or so years since we had been there and we'd had some fruit from them.

I didn't have the rose bush any more by then, though, sir. Even though it had done so well in Muswellbrook, the rose had never taken when we moved to Sydney and it died not long after we came to Botany. I was a good deal sorry for that because the Missus had given it to me, and when it died it was another piece of my other life gone, and I missed the pink roses.

29.

Michael was one of the only boarders that I brought into the house at Pople's Terrace, as most were brought home by Charles. I met Michael at the Amos's Pier Hotel one Saturday afternoon when Charles and the boarders were having their weekly baths.

By this time I had had my dear baby Charlie and that particular week him, May, Edwin, and Frederick had all been sick with colds and slept in my room, that I may better tend them through the night. Charles had slept in the sitting room with the older boys.

I myself had very little sleep that week and so, feeling the children were a little better and needing to escape the confines of the cottage while the men had their baths, I left all the children in the care of their father. The older boys would be bathing themselves and May could help with the baby, so I went out for a walk.

On bathing days, I could not go out to the swamp as I might have liked because the men would all be undressed at the back of the house. And so it was for most of the houses in that row, for Saturday afternoon was bath time right along the street. There were only a few walks which were decent for the women on a Saturday afternoon. I went to the hotel, which was only a few doors away.

I had no coin to speak of, for I had spent the last few pennies at Sayers's grocery store when I purchased some camphor oil to ease the children's chests, although Mr Sayers was a good grocer and often let me run on tick. The publican at the Amos's Pier Hotel knew me; he gave me the nod as I entered the lounge. I saw my friend Mary and her husband, William, sitting at a table with another gentleman who I did not know. William and the other gentleman were quite close in conversation and Mary gave me a wave and motioned for me to go and sit beside her, which I did.

She said, Are you not drinking then, Louisa? I told her I had no coin, having spent the last on the children while they were sick, and she said she would stand me a drink, for that was the way with our friendship, that we would share when the other was a bit short of coin. And though I may borrow, I always return.

You will not know Mary, sir, for she and William moved on to Melbourne shortly after I met Michael and she has not come to any of my trials.

I gladly accepted the drink and she said she would introduce me to her new friend. When the two men paused in their conversation, Mary said, Mr Collins, I would like to introduce you to my friend Louisa Andrews, and the gentleman turned and smiled at me, and said it was his pleasure to meet me. He was young and handsome and I thought so from the very first. And that was how I met Michael Collins, the man who would become my husband. The man they want to hang me for murdering.

I stop here.

Hang me, I think, will they really hang me?

Are you all right, Louisa?

I think I might like a drink of water, sir.

I would actually like to have something stronger, I think, but then there is no hope of that.

The water comes and I take a sip.

And so you met Michael Collins? the chaplain says.

Well, yes, sir, I say. I did. I asked Mary how she had met this new friend and she said she had met him on the tram coming out from Sydney. He had been at the races and was thinking of moving to Botany. Mary had been in to the fish market that morning, and he had come by way of the hotel to share a drink and meet her husband. Mary still had the fish wrapped and on the ground in her basket and nodded to the basket by means of showing me the fish. She need not have bothered, for fish from the market have a way of letting you know they are there without you having to see them.

I had been drinking my beer while she told me this story for I was mighty tired and thirsty after the long week, as I have told you. Presently, Michael Collins turned to me and noticed my glass was empty, and he asked if he might be permitted to stand me a drink, for, he said, he had had a good day at the cards and he was of a generous mind.

I said I had thought he had come by his winnings at the races and not at cards.

He told me he had winnings at both that day.

I said I would not have the means to repay him in turn and buy him a drink, for I had spent the last of my coin on medicine for my sick children, and he would be moved on before I had more money. And he said that it was a good woman who would forsake her own pleasure for the sake of her children and that such action was worthy of his generosity.

He said he would be buying Mary and her husband a drink as well.

I said I was a married woman and he should have no expectations and he would do well to remember that.

Then I let him buy me a drink.

30.

I am melancholy the next day because of Michael. I have been thinking back to the time we first met, and thinking of his face. He was so young and handsome that night.

31.

A doctor has come into my cell and says he will examine me.

I think it is a doctor who works at the prison hospital, but I cannot be sure. I am glad it is not one of the doctors who attended Michael or Charles, for I place no store by their medicine; none of their powders worked.

I do not know why this doctor has come, or how he will examine me. I wonder if the Female Governor has requested he come and visit, and give me some laudanum for my nerves. It might pass the time.

But he is not visiting me to give me laudanum.

When he arrives, Alice and I are sitting on the chairs, and Alice is reading aloud from the Bible.

I am too downhearted to read it myself. I can barely bother to listen. It is just droning.

We hear the key in the lock of the cell door, and the Female Governor comes in and a man is with her. I am a doctor, he says. I am here to examine you so please lie down, Mrs Collins.

For a moment, I do not understand him, and then he says again, Lie down, Mrs Collins, and the Female Governor gestures to the bed and so I lie down.

I am thinking of the Missus because she would lie down when the doctor came to visit, and he would give her laudanum. So I am still thinking this might be what he is going to do, and then I hear the doctor tell Alice to hold me down. Alice looks puzzled and the Female Governor says that she does not think this is needed, and the doctor says that he is the doctor and he will decide. And so Alice comes over to the bed and kneels down and places her hand upon my shoulder.

The Female Governor stands at the end of the bed.

The doctor asks me if I have had relations with any man since I killed my husband.

I am confused for a moment, and I cannot think of what he means – since I killed my husband?

He says, Have you, woman? I shake my head.

He tells Alice to hold me firmly and he kneels down on the floor. He reaches over and undoes the cord around my prison dress and lifts up the skirt. I think to protest but know I cannot and so I close my eyes and put my hands over my face. He pulls down my underthings and pokes and prods my stomach, and near that area of mine which is most personal. He puts his hands there in an intimate way.

I cannot see, and I do not want to, but I hear someone else enter the room through the open door. I know they are there for I hear the doctor speak to them.

As you can see, he says, she is not with child. I hear a few murmurs, and make out the word 'enough' and then I hear the Female Governor say, Have you finished yet, sir?

Her voice is shrill.

Then the doctor says he will leave me to the guards, and he gets up, and I hear footsteps leave the room.

Someone covers my modesty and pulls down my skirts.

I keep my eyes closed.

Then the Female Governor says, It is done now, Louisa.

I hear the cell door close, but I know Alice will remain, to sit on the chair and watch me.

I turn my head to the wall.

That Alice might not see my shame.

The Botany Murderess
Visited by Her Children

She is under the immediate charge of the female warders, who never relinquish their watch night or day, and all interviews with outsiders are carried on in her presence. The murderess eats, drinks, and sleeps remarkably well, and is chatty and affable to those around her to a degree. The Rev. Canon Rich, chaplain of the gaol, is unceasing in his visits, and in the care and solicitude he displays for the welfare of the unfortunate woman, and the many calls he makes appear to form pleasurable breaks in the monotony of her present existence. Up to the present time she has made no statement as to her guilt or otherwise, and occupies the whole of her day with reading and talking. Her children have already visited her since her condemnation, and the terrible position in which her mother is placed is most acutely felt by the fair-headed, tiny girl, May. This little thing wept most bitterly on her first visit, and was with difficulty removed from the cell and the termination of her interview ... Some few days ago a rumour was current to the effect that Louisa Collins was likely to become a mother. She was yesterday examined by the gaol surgeon (Dr. O'Connor), who has reported on the subject to the authorities. So far the result of his investigations has not been made known, but it is extremely probable that the conclusion arrived at will be a negative one. From the day on which sentence of death was passed upon Louisa Collins, her hopes for a reprieve have remained unaltered. She refuses to believe that the last dread punishment of the law will be carried into effect, and lives on, buoyed up by the most sanguine of hopes.

The Brisbane Courier[15]

32.

Canon Rich has asked me to visit with him this evening, and has said he might come to my cell, but I have told Alice I will not be able to attend him.

I find myself very low.

I ask Alice that she tell the chaplain I require my privacy in my cell.

Alice steps from my cell into the corridor and speaks with someone. I hear their voices, but I cannot make out the words.

There is no one guarding me in my cell. I may cause bedlam, given the freedom of being on my own.

But I do not. I lie upon my bed and I think back to that first meeting with Michael, and though I would not tell anyone this, that day was one of the happiest days of my life. I had left the confines of noisy chaos and sick children and I had walked into the hotel just a few steps along the road and yet it seemed as though I had walked into another world.

In meeting Michael I was Louisa once more – not a mother or a landlady or a wife – and it was as though the years of children and work and cooking and poverty had slipped away. A young, handsome man was offering to buy me a drink. And he was fancy with the words and used them to charm. I think I saw something in him that reminded me of Harry from my childhood. I knew from the first that Michael was a rogue with a smooth tongue, but on the night I met him I did not care, for I thought I would never see him again. Later, when we married and he was mine, I forgave him being a rogue because he had chosen me, above all others. This young, handsome man had chosen me.

I have wondered, since I have so much time to do so, how I came to be in this place, in this situation, and I know it is because of Michael. And I look back to the moment when we met and I ask if I had known how it would end, would I have done any differently, would I have said no to that drink?

I doubt it.

That first drink Michael bought me turned into several more, as Michael seemed to have plenty of money in his pocket.

Mary and William and Michael and I sat at the table for some time and we talked and laughed. Then my son Arthur came into the pub, looking for me, and I knew that Charles had sent him, for this was something he would do when he thought I had been too long away from the children. Arthur came to the table and said that Pa had told him to come and get me for it was time I should be getting dinner. Michael said what a fine strapping lad this boy of mine was, and I must have had him when I was very young, as I did not look old enough for such a son.

I laughed at his flattery and said for Arthur to tell his father I would be home directly and Arthur left. Then Michael said he wished he could have a woman like me to come at his beck and call, but I acted that I paid him no heed for I thought it to just be his way. Then he placed his hand upon mine, there, right at the table in front of the whole room, and he said I should have one more drink before I went. And so I did. Then, when I left, he said he hoped he would meet me again and would I be going to the hotel tomorrow night, for he thought he would seek lodgings nearby. I gave Mary a kiss and we giggled like young girls and then we parted in good company. As I left, Mary and William commenced singing, the fish long forgotten in its basket under the table.

When I got home Charlie was crying and the other children were wanting their supper. I put potatoes on and while they were boiling I took my little Charlie into the bedroom and sat with him on the bed and gave him some milk.

I sat feeding the baby and listening to the other children squabbling and Charles in the sitting room complaining that he should not have to do the work of a woman, occasionally placing his head around the door to tell me how disgraceful I was to be drunk and leaving a sick baby, and that I had no shame.

I sat on the bed, my head thumping, and all I thought upon was the time I had just spent in another world, as Louisa.

With Michael.

33.

If I am not reprieved, I know I will have few enough days left and so I tell myself I should not lose them being melancholy. The next day I visit with the chaplain. He comes to my cell.

I say, I have a picture of Michael for you to see, sir, for I have been thinking of him a great deal.

I keep the picture of Michael and me as it is the only photograph I have of him. I had to write to the Prison Governor specifically for permission to have the photograph. And when I had permission I asked someone familiar with my house if he might collect the photograph for me, and I told him exactly where he might find it.

I cannot see what harm it would be to have a photograph with me, can you, sir?

The chaplain says he cannot, particularly if the Governor has approved this.

Michael is handsome in his suit, although the trousers are the ones he would later wear in bed when he had his sore leg. I am shy at the camera.

We had married in St Silas's Church, the church near Waterloo station, and I had treated myself to a new dress and hat. And then when we decided to get a photograph taken, we wore our nice clothes from the wedding. I wore my gloves and a pair of small gold earrings and I had a parasol, so I did feel like a grand lady. And Michael wore his watch, although you can only see the chain in the photograph, but it was a very nice watch, sir.

I look at the photograph and think I must appear very different in the prison photographs, for here I have pretty hair and a lovely gown and hat. I had taken time with my appearance and worn warm rags in my hair to bed. I had greased my hands, as I used to do with the cattle fat back when Charles and I were in the butcher shops, so they were quite soft, although not as soft as I should have liked. I was careful to wash my face well and apply a bit of soot from the fire to heighten my eyelashes and some flour upon my skin to ease off the brown. When I look at this photograph, it belongs to another time for they are all gone – my Michael and his watch, my hat and gloves, my dress.

Perhaps I should have been in mourning black for a year after the death of my husband Charles, but I chose not to wear full mourning for him as I have never worn full for my children when they died. I had no money for such a luxury when my Ernest died and so it did not feel proper to wear mourning for David, and in any case I had a great dislike of mourning and wearing black on account of the Missus.

And I am told they have talked about this in the papers, about my not wearing black and how it was unseemly. But then they would not know the half of it, would they?

I mourned for my husband Charles in my own way, although in truth our marriage was not a happy one and I cannot pretend otherwise. Charles was joyless, as some men can be. We did not get off to a good start, for he did not court me, and there was not much effort on his part, and I always resented that.

It is true that I cannot say I miss his laugh or wit, sir, for he rarely shared these with me. But now, when I think back on Charles, I remember as how he was a good father, and tried to be a good provider, and how he worked hard. And I think upon the trip we shared on the road to Sydney. That was a happy time between us and full of possibilities for the future.

No, sir, I do not have a photograph of Charles.

34.

I do not tell the chaplain that the first night I met Michael I thought the night would pass and that I would not see him again, and so perhaps I had felt free to laugh with him and enjoy the warmth of the beer and the company, for what harm could come of it?

Then, several days later, I saw my friend Mary. I sought her out at the hotel on the pretence of repaying her for the drink she had bought me. I asked after Michael and she said she had not seen him since that night and she did not think he was in the area, as he had not found the work he was seeking.

I remember my heart dropping, but I thought, It is just as well as I am a married woman and I need to be happy with my lot. Yet I found that the more I thought of Michael, the more disappointed I became in my life with Charles, but it was only a whim, and I thought it would pass.

The Saturday next I spent some time with Mary, but had only had the couple of drinks and was preparing to head home when Michael came into the bar and began to talk with another man.

I did not want to appear eager to see him, although I was so. I sat talking with Mary and before long he came over to our table and asked if he might sit.

Well, I said, he might.

He enquired after the health of my children and I told him they were much improved, thank you very much.

He said I looked well myself and I blushed.

He told me he was late arriving to the hotel as he had been to Randwick and playing the horses that day.

He said he sometimes worked for a bookie, because the bookie thought he was pleasant on the eye for the ladies, and with that he looked at me and winked.

I asked what sort of racetrack it was that ladies attended, and he said there were many women who went, hanging off the fellas, and picking out the horses for them to bet upon, and always picking the horse because it was a pretty colour or flicked its tail at her.

Then the toffs would try to act like big men and place their own bets and 'throw in a bob' on the horse the lady had liked. That was when Michael's role came in, and the bookie would nod and Michael would smile at the woman and say she was a good judge of horse flesh and make no mistake, and surely the lady's selection was worth a few more coins?

He tried those words on me as he said them and we laughed at how convincing he would be. He said the ladies would flutter their eyelashes and the toffs, wanting to appear rich, and being jealous of this young man, would bring out a few more coins. Some would end up spending pounds on the bet, and more often than not the horse was a dumb nag with no hope in the race and so the bookie would collect more profit. On a good day he would give plenty of this to Michael.

Mary and I laughed at the nature of it.

We have often thought we could clean up even better, Michael said. How so? Mary asked. Well, by entering a pretty pony into the race, one with no hope of winning, he said. All the women love a pretty pony.

Mary and I laughed and though I knew I were being played like one of the ladies at the races, I blushed at the thought of it.

He went on to more talk. Of course, he himself would have the tip on what was the best nag in the race, and if he placed a bet he would often clean up, as they say, with a profit from the venture.

With that he took from his pocket a wad of notes, round and fat, and told us that it had been a good day and he had taken over twenty pounds.

I tried to contain my expression, but I had not seen so much money in a good long while.

He said this meant he would not need to work for some time, and now all he needed to do was to find a place to stay, for he had a likening to stay in Frog's Hollow.

Mary said she was sure she did not know why he would stay in a rat's hole such as this, what with the smell of the fellmongers and the noise of the brickworks. And he said granted this was perhaps not the most scenic of places, but there were other delights which he chose to look at instead.

He looked at me as he said it.

And though I was a married woman, I did not lower my head or blush, and I saw Mary's smile upon her face.

35.

I tell the chaplain, when we next visit together, that I began to go to the hotel more often as it was no fun at home with Charles. He and I argued more than ever, for he said I was drinking too much and that he would be off working and I would do nothing and he did not like coming home with no dinner prepared and the children being cared for by the neighbour and me off at the hotel. I thought this most unfair and said so to him as, I said, I was cook and cleaner and mother to everyone in the house – child, husband and boarder alike.

I said I liked to have a few drinks with people who enjoyed my company and be myself for a time and he would say what about the children and that might have been well when I was a young girl, but I was a grown woman now, with a family and responsibilities, and I should behave better.

We would try to argue without the boarders hearing, for we did not want them to move out. We had whispered arguments in our bedroom, and the words would become spiteful as they grew softer, I am ashamed to say. For if you are screaming, you will be mindful of the words everyone can hear, but if you are quieter you will say such vicious things. And when we argued like this, we were very unkind to each other.

I liked to pretend that the boarders could not hear the arguments but I know they could, for the walls were none too thick, and we could hear all the comings and goings in the other houses and so I understood that they would be able to hear ours as well. But we did try to keep our voices low for decorum's sake.

One of the neighbours, although I will not say which one, sir, who lived up the road, would throw things at her husband and scream like her throat was being cut, and this for all the world to hear. Often a crowd would gather to listen to the row, and you could stand upon the street as though it were a penny sideshow – one of the Punch and Judys which you would see up town for tuppence, for there might be windows smashing and pots hurling and goodness knows what else. Someone would end up going for the constable and then he would come and quieten them down by threatening to arrest one or the other, and it was funny to watch because then the couple would nearly always turn on him and say he had no right to interfere in their marriage.

One night, I came home from the hotel and Charles and I had one of our arguments and one of our boarders came and told us to stop our quarrelling or he would be off and go down the road to board at number five. Well, as you can imagine I did not take kindly to being told off by a boarder in my own house, and I told this man so, and the boarder said some rude words to me, and Charles said – and I thank him for this – he said the man should not speak to me in this way and unless he apologised, he could leave. The boarder said he would leave that very night, and Charles said good riddance to him and all, and would he like Charles to help him pack, and the man stormed off and out the door. I thought that would be the end of our quarrel for the night, but when the boarder left, Charles turned on me.

He shouted at me that I needed to stop drinking and I needed to be a better mother and wife, and I said things in return which were hurtful and unkind and which I now regret sadly on account of Charles being dead.

Towards the end of the argument, when we had both run out of being bothered, Charles said we must find a new boarder to take the place of the one we had just lost, and I said I already had someone in mind.

And that was how Michael came to live in our home.

36.

The words came out of my mouth before I had really thought them through, for it was one thing to have some drinks and fun with a handsome charmer who was a bit of a rogue, and another to have him move into your home and live under the same roof as you and your husband.

Michael was so different to Charles, and I couldn't help myself but to want to have more time with him, especially after Charles told me off for needing to grow up and be a better wife and mother.

You see, sir, Michael liked me for being Louisa, but I felt I was always a wife or mother or shopgirl or landlady to Charles, and not good enough at any of these jobs. I suppose in meeting Michael I saw the glimpse of the woman I might have been if I had not married young and had so many children.

It took me about a week to find Michael for even though I went the few doors up to the hotel several times a day, he did not ever seem to be there. And that whole week I was asking myself whether it was a good idea to have this man under my roof and whether he would still think of me as fun if he lived in my house, or if he too would think I should be a better wife and mother.

During the week I was looking for him, I gave the cottage a good clean so as to have it nice for when he came. I got to and washed the fly mess off the windows, and banged the mats out upon the road, and I moved the couch and swept floors and put the curtains aside to be washed on the following Monday. I cleaned the kitchen and Charles saw me cleaning and commented how tidy the house was. He was never one to apologise, but I took his compliment by way of apology, and we came to some sort of truce for our bad words to each other. He offered to help me and so he cleaned the cooker, for it had an opinion of its own and would like to spit out at me when I used it. He chopped wood and stacked it neatly, and so all in all the cottage and the backyard had a fine box of kindling, split nice and fine for starting the fire. There was always plenty of kindling, for the swamp tea trees out the back had ample bark.

It was at this time that I saw the damage the rats had done to the stuffing in our mattress. There was stuffing on the floor and rat droppings under the bed.

I went to the corner store and bought a roll of brown paper and I already had some Rough on Rats. It was what we had used in the butcher shops as Cook had recommended it, although she was very careful and did not keep it anywhere near her sugar, for she told the story of the wife who put it in her husband's milksops instead of sugar and when he tasted it and asked why it was so bitter, he fell down dead. Though we mainly used block sugar, it being cheaper, I was always careful, mindful of Cook's story.

There are always rats where there is industry and butchering, for it is the blood which will attract them, make no mistake, and though we had them as a problem in the butcher shops, I have never got used to them; they are sly creatures. And they say there are some big rats' nests in Botany and there are certainly plenty of rats, and we always saw them at night when we walked out on the street, but when I realised that the rats were coming into the house I was fearful for my babies. So I spread the Rough on Rats around, and placed the box where the children could not reach, and was careful that I kept it well away from the sugar.

I did not ever sprinkle the powder about on the floor or under the bed when we still had babes crawling on the floor. They might get it upon their hands, and babies are always putting their hands into their mouths.

I put some of the powder in a piece of brown paper and tucked this up under the bed between the frame and the mattress, in a similar fashion to how I had used it in the days when we were first married and we had such problems with rats in the butcher shop and our hut. The brown paper was wedged up behind the mattress and close to the wall, where a crawling baby might not find it. Later that day, when Charles came home from work, I showed him where I had put the packet of powder and what it was and I told him of the rats in the mattress, and he agreed with me that the baby was not likely to find it there. He would tell you this himself, sir, if he was able.

I put some of the powder high upon the beam in the privy and then I stored the box away, so as to have some should I need more.

If the judges at the trials had asked me, I could have said why I kept Rough on Rats, and why most of the good wives of Sydney would have it in their houses.

The chaplain reads a few passages from the Bible and then I walk back to my cell with the warders.

While I walk back, I am thinking how I was cleaning the house extra because of Michael, and how it took me nearly a week to find him. I had almost given up hope, as I had even taken the tram a few stops along and went to a different pub up the road, enquiring after Michael Collins, and they had scoffed at me and said surely every second Irishman was called Michael Collins and the others were called Robert Emmet and how many did I want? Just the one, I said, and we had a laugh.

And then I found him. He returned to the Amos's Pier Hotel. I walked in and he gave me a wave and my heart did skip a beat, for he looked so handsome. I walked over to him and he placed his hand upon my arm. Louie, he said. I hear you have been seeking me.

Well, my heart filled so I thought it might burst, for he called me by my own name, and a pet one he had made for me, and for a moment I was Louisa again, not Mrs Collins or Ma or the landlady.

But I will not tell Canon Rich those things.

37.

When I next see the chaplain, he starts with a prayer for me, and when he finishes he says he has written this out and would I like to have the piece of paper, so I can pray this particular prayer in my cell.

I say, Thank you, sir, I will place this in the Bible.

He is most attentive to me, and I wonder that he has the time, for there are hundreds of prisoners in this gaol.

But then I suppose they are not all condemned to die.

I begin to think upon this, and perhaps my face shows that I do.

The chaplain asks me to continue my story about Michael.

Well, sir, I say, I found him and I asked Michael if he was still seeking lodgings and he said he was, and I said I might have some which would be suitable and he gave a grin and made a remark, for that was his way, to speak in a cheeky manner.

We made arrangements for Michael to come to Pople's Terrace the next day, around ten o'clock in the morning. I chose the time as Charles would be at work, and Michael could settle in.

I waited on my doorstep, looking to the road and checking

as the time ran past ten o'clock. Mrs Law saw me upon my front step and wished me a good morning and I greeted her and she remarked how well I looked on that morning and I asked her, Do I? For, I said, I had done nothing of any consequence for my appearance to change. And she enquired after Herbert, for he had recently taken work away up north and I said he was doing very well, although I missed having him at home.

I said how it had been a fine crisp morning and would no doubt be a beautiful day. Then, over her shoulder, I could see Michael walking across the little footbridge which marks the entrance to Frog's Hollow and he was wearing his suit and carrying a case.

Michael approached and dipped his hat and said, Good morning, Mrs Andrews, I have come about the room as I was told you have one available. And then he turned to Mrs Law and asked of me, Who is your charming friend? He said this, cool as you like.

Good morning, Mr Collins. This is Mrs Law, I said. My neighbour.

Michael turned on the charm to her.

He placed his small case on the ground and offered her his hand. Michael Collins, Mrs Law. My pleasure to meet you, he said. And it is a fine morning and lovely to see two neighbours enjoying the sunshine together.

Mrs Law then said, And a pleasure to meet you too, sir, and I am thinking you would be Irish with a name like Michael Collins, but I do not detect the brogue in your voice.

No, said Michael. I am a native of Victoria. Although perhaps one of my grandfathers — now there would be an Irish accent for you. They continued on in this manner with Michael giving all the charm and Mrs Law lapping it up, for he could be smooth, my Michael.

May came out from the cottage with young Charlie in her

arms, saying he was fussing and so I must give him my attention, and though I was thinking that May just wanted to see what was happening and who this man was, I said excuse me to Michael and Mrs Law and turned to the children.

I did not want the neighbours gossiping that I would neglect my children for this new boarder or Charles hearing such tales before Michael even started in the house. So, I addressed the baby's needs, and when I returned Mrs Law was laughing at something Michael was saying and tipping her head back as she did. I stood at the door of the cottage for a moment, with the baby upon my hip, and I watched the two of them chatting quite amiably as though they were friends of long standing.

Michael was saying all the things Mrs Law wanted to hear.

Had I had any thoughts that way, I might have been jealous at his talk, but I was a married woman, sir, and so I did not. And besides, he saw me standing in the doorway and while she talked away and was pointing out some landmark down the street, he gave me a wink and so I knew he was just playing along.

Then he said he really must be getting on and seeing the room, and he hoped it would be suitable and he would see her soon. He dipped his hat and came into the parlour.

It was only myself and May and young Charlie home that morning. May would normally be in school but I had kept her home that day so that she might help me with the baby.

When Michael came into the cottage he spoke first to May and said what a pretty girl she was, and so good to be helping care for her younger brother, and I could see he was being a charmer to her just as he had done with Mrs Law.

Michael asked May if she might give him the tour of the house, and she was all talk telling him, And this is the dining table and the back door, and went about showing him through the cottage and yard.

I believe it was then, that first afternoon, that I began to imagine what life might be like if Michael were my husband and not Charles. But that was just a fancy of mine, sir; at the time, I never thought such a thing would happen.

Charles did not meet Michael that day, as Michael had already left by the time Charles got home from work. Michael said he needed to go and collect another suit from a former lodging. I thought it odd that he did not bring all his clothes with him as he knew he would be moving, but I later came to realise that Michael had his own particular ways about him.

Before he left, Michael placed five pounds upon the mantelshelf over the fireplace and said that would be a guarantee that he would return.

When Charles came home he came in around the back, as was his way when he was returning from work, for his clothes were often filthy with blood and wool. He wore a leather apron but it did little to keep him clean. And then there was the smell.

Do you know the sheep smell, sir? They stink badly enough when they are alive, as any shearer's wife will tell you, but when they are dead it is as though all their final stench goes into their wool during their last moments upon Earth, for they reek twice as bad once they are dead.

I always had two copper boilers set up out the back for the smelly work clothes, for it would save me the burden of going to the pump each day and filling the copper with fresh water, which I had to do when I washed on a Monday. Charles would soak his filthy sheep clothes in the water so that the flies would not get into the cloth. Then he would walk to the pump from which we drew our water.

That afternoon when Charles called hello to me from out the back and I looked out the kitchen window and saw him place his shirt in the copper, then walk down to the pump, I thought how old he looked. I had never found Charles very attractive, though I do not like to speak badly of those who have passed, and he had many other good qualities as I have told you previous.

But as I watched Charles lift the flannel and clean off the dirt, I could see the age upon his body, the folds under his neck and the slackness under his arms. And I thought of Michael, and how smart and strong he had looked in his suit. I know it is wicked to have such thoughts, sir.

Charles finished his wash and came into the kitchen and asked if he might meet the new boarder. May said he had gone somewhere and would be back later.

Then it was May herself who went to the mantel in the parlour and got the five pounds for Charles.

A fancy man, is he? Charles asked May.

May shrugged, as I do not think she knew what her pa meant.

Then he said to me, Young and handsome, this friend of yours is, is he? I said Michael had come into some money with luck on the cards and that he was just an acquaintance who paid his rent in advance.

I turned back to the stew I was making, knowing that five pounds was a lot of money and thinking that in preparing the cottage for Michael's arrival I had run up a tick at Sayers's store. I would use the money to settle the account.

38.

All was well for some time. Michael had not yet started work at the fellmongers, but he went off somewhere each afternoon and came home very late. So Charles would be up and gone before Michael woke, and in bed before he came home. This went on for several days without the two men meeting each other.

I could not tell you what it was Michael did for work at that time, sir, but I think he was off gambling. I tried to keep the house quiet as best I could as he would rise about midday. He would go down to the pump to make himself fresh.

Then later, when he was going out, he would take his suit from the nail and ask if he might dress in the children's room for, he said, there was a looking glass in there, and he took great care with his appearance.

And I suppose I took more time with my own appearance and I made an effort to sweep out our cottage and pretty it as best I could as I had made such an effort to have it nice. I was on the lookout for the rats who had been in our house. I found two of them dead and so I did not put down any more of the powder, but kept the box of it upon the shelf in case it was needed.

Michael and Charles were cordial enough when they did meet each other, which, as I said, was after Michael had been boarding for a few days on account of Charles working in the day and Michael working – or at least going out – at night. Charles treated him as he would any of the other boarders. Which was all he was at the time, sir.

When Michael said he needed work in the daytime as he had lost his work in the evenings – although I was never entirely sure what it was he did, but whatever it was, he did it no more – it was Charles who got Michael work at the local fellmongering factory and they seemed very friendly together. Michael did not keep that particular job for long, although I cannot recall on what account.

With so many of us crowded into the one house, and me working to try to keep the house in order and the children fed, I began to think that Michael's earlier attentions would wane. It could not be more obvious to him that I was a married woman, for he now lived in close company with me and my husband. As the days went into weeks, I learnt Michael was a great tease, and a flirt, and he would tell me I was a sweetie, and a rose, and he would be winking at me, although I never placed much store by his flirtations, for I knew his type. Oh, he was a rogue, and I thought his teasing and flirting to all be in jest, but the fun continued, sir. Now, it is one thing to say a few teasing words when you are enjoying the drink with a friend, and another to continue to enjoy their company when you hear them screaming at their children, or see them doing the washing or coming from the privy in the morning, which is what occurs when you live in the same house with someone.

But he did make me laugh, and he continued to do so, even with all the children and boarders and noise of the household. And so it was that I began to think we were good friends, for the teasing was of a manner that good friends might do to each other.

Michael did not take to factory work and would be at Pople's Terrace more during the day, when he was between jobs. He still had the money to pay his board, although I could not say how he came by this. Then it was that one of the other boarders – although I shall not say which one, for I do not want to even say his name, it makes me so angry, so I shall say just one of the boarders – told Charles that he thought I was particular with Michael. Even though I always had one of the children home with me during the day, as I said, to make it look proper.

Charles asked me if this were true and I said it was not and that Michael and I were friends and that was all, and I said he should know me for the faithful wife I was and he should not believe the gossip of one of our boarders. And he said he wanted to know what went on in his own house, and I said if he wanted to put a boarder's word over that of his wife, then perhaps he would prefer to be married to him. Charles tried to hush me, saying that the boarder would hear, and I said I hoped that he did, spreading such lies as that about me. And, well, I will not tell you the rest, but some very unpleasant words were said.

From that time, I did not speak to this boarder at all, and Charles did not speak to Michael, and watched him like a hawk, so it was not a happy household.

Legislative Assembly

Mr. WALKER urged that the State was just on the eve of committing a national murder, and asked that justice should be tempered with mercy. Capital punishment never had a deterrent effect, and imprisonment for life would meet the justice of this case ...

Mr. NEILD contended that the little children who gave evidence in the case were brought to the court time after time until they became educated up to the matter ...

Mr. NEILD said he did not mean to say that the officers of the Crown tutored the children, but that these little children could not be brought so often into the court without the matter being impressed on their minds. He could not better explain what he meant than by saying that a person by repeating a lie often came eventually to believe it ...

Sir HENRY PARKES said that he believed that the women of the country would vote for Mrs. Collins being hanged.

The Sydney Morning Herald[16]

39.

With all the arguing and unhappiness after the boarder's nasty gossip, I began to think of how sorry my lot in life was. I began to resent Charles, as he was no fun at all, although that is not something I should be saying, sir, because of what happened after.

After the boarder made his coarse remarks, Michael and I became secretive with our friendship, where it had been all out and in the open previous – our jokes and talking and the like. We wanted to have fun so we would go down to the hotel after Charles had gone to bed and have a drink and talk there. Michael had found other work carting green skins from the slaughterhouses on Glebe Island to the fellmongering sheds at Botany, so he and Charles were rising and leaving for work about the same time. I know the work was hard, and Charles would go to bed early, being tired, but Michael was able to stay up much later and still get up early, him being so much younger, and Michael only worked a few days here and there, whereas Charles worked every shift he could.

Michael told me he grew up on a sheep farm near Ballarat and was used to working with sheep and sheep skins. That was why he had come to work at Botany – he had heard the best fellmongers worked there and he wanted to learn their skills. And that was why he did not need to work every shift he was offered, or so he told me. And not working long hours also gave Michael the opportunity to be gambling. Now, I know Charles did not approve of this as he did not consider gambling a steady form of income, and neither was it, as it turned out.

When he went out to the gamble, I would loan Michael back the rent money, for as he explained to me, he liked to pay his rent when the cards were kind, but he might need to borrow it back when Lady Luck was looking away. I did not like to give him back his money as I thought the other boarders might think that they too would be able to loan back their money – we had two other boarders at the time – and also I knew Charles would not like it. One time when Charles asked where the money from the rent jar had gone, I said I had used it to pay off Sayers's grocery tick, but this was only partly true and telling a lie to my husband weighed heavily upon me, and he need have only asked Mr Sayers to find me out.

So the next time he asked, I told the truth and said I had given money to Michael to use for his trip to the races. Charles was angry and he said that the money was not mine to give and was no longer Michael's to have, and did I not know I was taking food from the mouths of my own children?

Charles said he would turn all of the boarders out of the house as he said there was no money coming in from them, for it was just given back whenever they liked so that they might go and gamble and so there was no point in them being kept in our home and they were to be off. And Charles said he was sick of all the gossip besides. And so I said that if he kicked out Michael because of the gossip of a boarder, and me lending a friend some money, then he might tend to his own filthy washing for I was having none of it. And so we argued over whose house it was, because yes he paid the rent and earnt the money, but I did work that was not paid. He said I had never worked a day in my life and I drank all his money away at the pub, but who was it that cooked the meals and washed the clothes and cared for the children? I suppose this argument is one many women must have with their husbands, for it is they who get the coin for their work, and we who do not.

I promised not to lend Michael back the rent money but Charles was having none of it. And all the boarders left that night, every one of them, even Michael. But there was no fighting between Michael and Charles that night. That came only a short time later. And it was a dreadful row, right in the middle of the street.

40.

I had caught the tram into the centre of Sydney with the children for no particular reason other than a nice outing for the day.

We made our way up Elizabeth Street and we sat in the park. Frederick and May and Edwin and baby Charlie played among the flowers. On account of it being near to Christmas the city had placed a large tree in the centre of the park and decorated it with coloured paper and the like, just as the royal family do, them being German.

It was a hot afternoon and after a time sitting watching them, I left the children to play and sought out the refreshment tent.

I bought a nobbler of beer and turned to look for a seat.

And there was Michael.

We shared some drink in the refreshment tent and then when the time came to leave, Michael caught the same tram back to Frog's Hollow with me and the children.

On the way back to the house, Michael and I bought some beer and as we sat and shared a drink Michael told me his bookmaker friend had gone to Queensland and Michael was thinking of following him as he had no work.

I said that I did not want him to go because he was my friend and, well, we spoke of our friendship.

It was a sin, I know, and I confess I gave in to the weakness which he presented. I am but a weak woman, sir, and one who had gone without such loving for some time. We had been drinking for the afternoon, and the children were happy having been taken to the park.

Perhaps it was the joy of the coming season, or the thought that he would go to Queensland, I do not know, but I sat beside him on the couch and we leant in together and kissed and I am ashamed to say it was in this intimate state that Charles found us when he came home. There I was, a married woman, who was kissing a man not her husband.

You will have heard the story of this day, sir, for it was the argument which was spoken of at the trials and I think it has been in the papers.

There was a terrible row between the two men. Charles took his fists to Michael and hit him and kicked him out into the street and then gave him a beating. And he used very bad language, the likes of which I had not heard Charles use before. Charles hit Michael right there in the road until there were bruises and blood upon his face. The neighbours all came out to watch as they fought. None of the men tried to break up the fight, although it was largely one-sided, as Charles was older but he was angry and strong, and we argued in the street like common folk, like a mob of dogs arguing over scraps, and it was shameful.

I screamed at Charles to stop and said Michael had only come back to ask if he might move back as a boarder and if he did not let Michael move back in to board, then I would run away to Queensland with him.

And Charles shouted that he would let that man back in his house over his own dead body, which as it turned out, was a very unfortunate thing to say. Then I went to Michael, who was lying on the ground and had his hands up to shield his face, and Charles stopped his punching as I knew Charles would not hit when there was a chance he might hit me. He was not a man who would ever hit a woman.

So Charles stopped.

I helped Michael to his feet and he gathered his things and said he would be on his way, but he was badly beaten and I would have liked him to come into the house, but did not dare ask him on account of Charles.

Our son Arthur took hold of his father then and asked him why he was fighting and Charles said that it did not concern him, but Arthur persisted, I suppose because fighting was very out of character for Charles. Then Charles said to Arthur that we – and here Charles pointed to Michael and me – wanted Charles out of the way.

The words have taken a different turn now, on account of Charles being dead, for what Charles meant was that we wanted him to stay out of the way so we might run away to Queensland together and that we were planning to do that very thing. But as it appears in the retelling, well, it sounds as though it means something else, because of Charles dying.

At the time of the fight, Charles also said he would like to see Collins provide for me as well as he had done for so many years and I laughed at him and said it was a joke and hadn't we taken in boarders because we had no money and his wages couldn't provide? But I should say, sir, that while Charles did not provide as well as I would have liked in our marriage, he did work very hard and one should remember the good in people, as we wish the good in us to be remembered also.

After the fight, Michael went off up the street and I said to Charles that if he did not let Michael stay, then Michael would go to Queensland for there was nothing surer, and I would go with him. For there was nothing left for me here with him and Charles may raise the children himself and see how he liked tending to all their needs. And I said some unkind words, which thankfully Arthur did not hear and which I do regret now.

It is often the way, isn't it, sir, that you say things in the heat of an argument and it is only the warmth of your temper which makes you say them. But then you cannot take them back when you calm down.

I went to see Constable Jeffes for I had some acquaintance with him as his beat would pass our door, and he would pop his head inside the cottage and he would say hello. I considered him a good copper and my friend. Well, I went to see Constable Jeffes to tell him that my husband had been fighting and had beaten one of our boarders, Michael Collins. I did not go into all the particulars myself, and I knew the neighbours would tell the constable soon enough about the argument.

The constable came and spoke with Charles and then he went and found Michael and asked if there was any need to take the matter further.

They say in the papers that there was a kicking out of the boarder, but there was certainly much more to it than that, for when Constable Jeffes sought out Michael he had a bruised face, which was plain to see, and though he did not show me, I think he may have shown the constable that he was bruised about the back and legs.

Michael did not press charges.

And he did not go to Queensland.

41.

My May comes to visit me today and sees me in my new cell.

She comes with someone from the government and I think it is this woman who has been appointed her guardian and is looking after May while I am in here.

Her hair is brushed and her dress is clean, but May herself looks very thin and carries a worried expression upon her face.

I want to speak with her, but I find I cannot find the words to say, and she looks around her. I think we are both low. We hold each other and then we both just give in to crying.

Later, we ease our tears and speak.

I ask her about her evidence, for I think speaking against me in court weighs heavily on the child. She says that now she is not sure about what she said in the court, and she did not know why she had ever said some of the things she did.

I look to Alice as May says this, and it is clear that she has heard the child. The guardian has a look of surprise upon her face too, but they neither of them say anything.

Then May starts crying again and says she thought she had got it wrong when she spoke in court, and she felt bad that the lawyers made so much of her words that they gave the thought to the jury that I was guilty. But, she says, the lawyers asked her so many times about everything that she got confused and had not known what to say in the end.

Then, between her sobs, May asks me if she has caused me to be hung, because she said the wrong thing. I hug her and say that if this does happen it will be because of the men in court and the government and not because of my little May, because she is only a child.

But I think if May changes her story, then they can never find me guilty.

Then the guardian steps forward and says it is time to be leaving, and I ask for a few more minutes, for pity's sake, and she steps back. I keep hugging May and her sobbing eases, and I say that I would like her to come to see me again soon and I kiss her goodbye.

As soon as she leaves I ask that I might go to the chaplain and write a letter.

I write to ask the Governor that May be allowed to talk to the judge, for she is now not sure of her testimony.

In the House

Wednesday was largely occupied by the affair of Louisa Collins, whose method of procuring a divorce by means of arsenic is open to serious objection.

The Sydney Morning Herald[17]

42.

After his fight with Michael, Charles and I were very unhappy, sir, and then there was Christmas, and we trudged on into the new year.

But it was really only some six weeks after their argument that Charles became sick and it was as though his very saying of the words that we wanted him out of the way had placed a curse upon him.

His illness began slowly. Charles came home from work earlier than usual one afternoon, having left complaining of a sore belly. It was most unlike him to be unwell, as he was known for being a good worker and reliable. He came home that day and spent time in the privy, then he took to his bed and, while there, he vomited several times.

I remember clearly the day Charles first got really sick because he had planned to be killing a pig. Now, I did not like it when he killed the pigs for he would slit their throats and they would gurgle their last scream as the blood gushed out of them. And we had lost money in Muswellbrook because of a pig.

But since we had moved to Botany, Charles had taken more

to killing them than beasts, because he could handle one on his own, whereas killing a beast was more difficult and required a gun to shoot the beast in the head, dead centre – they have such thick skulls, sir – and we did not have a crush or the equipment needed and nowhere to hang a beast. Charles had a small pen for the pig and he would let it roam in the swamp, and then when it got to a certain size he would kill it.

On the day that he was going to be killing the pig, Charles had a pain in the stomach and he was vomiting and had a bad bowel, which was most unpleasant. He was still able to get to the privy though, and so most of his being unwell was occurring in there, but of course he was not able to kill the pig.

By the next day he had taken to his bed, and he really did not get up from there again, sir.

There are those who are so often unwell they take delight in it and like to share their aches and pains with the world, describing every incident to others. Mrs Malone was like that, and she would have gladly described every piece of phlegm which ever came from her, should you care to ask. But Charles was not someone who took to illness, and in the time we had been together I can only recall he had been unwell on a small few occasions.

This time, I first thought he might have the influenza, or a sickness on account of the swamp across the road, for in the years we had lived at Botany there had been more and more people come to live in Frog's Hollow and whenever there is a crowd of people there are often sicknesses and more privies. And on occasion people would be sick and would blame the swamp, but I really did not know, sir, and that was why I later sent for the doctor.

Charles's taking to his bed and my needing to nurse him called something of a truce between us and gave us some opportunity to reconcile. It is often the way that things are forgiven when someone becomes ill.

Yet even after taking to his bed, Charles did not improve and so I sent someone on the tram to Elizabeth Street to ask the doctor to call, which he did late that night. He examined Charles and it was Charles himself who spoke with him and said he had pain and was very unwell with vomiting, and the doctor did not seem overly alarmed. He prescribed a mixture of certain powders. I cannot tell you what they were, for I never read the piece of paper, just handed it with some coin to one of the children and asked them to get the paper made up by the chemist. And I said if the chemist failed to attend, they were to knock on the door until they did, for I felt that the doctor would know best for my husband, or else there was no need for me to send for him to come at all, and there was the expense of his visit besides.

When the powders came, I mixed the medicine in a small glass, as the doctor had directed, and I gave this to Charles. But he did not seem to improve much, although he no longer had upset bowels.

The next day Charles was no better and if anything he was in greater pain, beyond the pain in his stomach. I tried to give him some milk and cod liver oil, but he refused as he said it tasted bitter. I said it might settle his stomach, but he said he did not want it.

And as he was not one of those who are often sick, I was surprised at his condition and not really sure as what to do and the house was full of people, all giving their opinion, and I am sure it was well meant, but it made me very confused. Mr Collis, Mr Kneller and the other neighbours were coming in several times a day, and this was good for Charles as he seemed to be interested in their news and he asked kindly after their own wives and children. And no one could give any advice as to why he was sick and none of the medicine the doctor said to use seemed to make him any better.

Charles disliked being idle for he had always been an active man. By that time, he could not make it out to the privy and I was needing to tend to him in that way and wash him and for a man such as my husband Charles, well, he found that very improper.

He did not improve.

He had hardly slept through the night and was tired and so after I had fixed the breakfast – although he himself ate nothing, I fed the children before sending them out to the neighbours – I sat down beside him and I remember it was just us in the room, which was uncommon, as at that time, between the neighbours coming to see how Charles was and the children, it seemed that the house was always full. But I remember that we were alone, for Charles said he would like to tell me of something in private. And it was then that he told me of his life insurance policy.

43.

Charles said that some years earlier a man selling life insurance had come to the factory where Charles was working at the time, and that this man had told all of the workers about an insurance policy they could take out to safeguard their families. The man had asked the workers how their children would survive if they themselves were not around to provide for them, and Charles had decided that he would sign up for the policy.

When Charles was telling me this, he could not recall the actual date he had first begun this arrangement and he said he had told me of it at the time, but I could not recall him ever mentioning it, sir. The lawyers and the papers say I killed Charles for his money, but why would I do this when I knew nothing of this insurance money until after Charles became sick?

And it was Charles himself, when he was sick, who asked me to see the insurance man to make sure all was in order with his life insurance, although there is no one else who can confirm this, I do not think. So, I made the ride into the city, catching the tram to the insurance office.

The man at the insurance office said that if my husband was

ill I should look that his will was in order, because even though Charles said his life insurance money would come to me, it would be best to have this confirmed in a will. I said that I did not know if Charles had a will as I did not think that the poorer people needed such things and it was only those grander folk with their estates and entailments and such who needed to think of wills. But the insurance man said Charles should have one and he arranged the wording of it, and he sat with me asking the details of our property and if we owned a house and land or livestock, and I was most humbled because I had no such property as he was asking. And I thought of how we used to have King and the wagon and the butcher shop, and now we only had some furniture, which I described to him, and some small amount of money in the savings which Charles had at the bank, although I was not sure of the exact amount of that, sir.

I felt very poor as I sat in the big office in that building. I do not know if you have seen them, but they are all marble and shiny and grand as though you might be in a palace, and it is plain to see where it is that the money you might store in a bank or insurance goes – on building luxury such as this. Each of the teller sections had a gas light and here I was sitting at a grand table, talking of our furniture – the kitchen table and the few chairs, and the settle which sat in the parlour, and our bed, and the dresser which sat under the window, and the beds of our children – and I asked the gentleman if I should include the washing copper and the pots and pans in the kitchen, for I still had the good teapot from the Missus and the frying pan from Cook. He said he did not think so. Then I asked if I should mention the paintings upon the walls and he said what type were they and I said one was from the Missus and she had given it to me when we first set up home, and he said he did not think so, and so I did not tell him of the ones which were on the wall and which came from the paper and showed sheep stations and pictures of grand houses.

I sat there and I thought that I did not have very much, even after all the years of marriage. And I looked down at my hands and I did not even have gloves upon them, as you were supposed to when you came into town. I thought back to my days cleaning the house for the Missus, and touching the pretty things and thinking I should have a house like that one day, and now I did not have it and my husband was ill and I would have no one to feed all my children.

And I began to cry a little, and the man gave me a gentle smile and said though he did not think the will would be needed because my husband would soon be well, he would write the will out himself and make sure he wrote it all proper and then all I would need to do was have two men witness Charles signing it. If he thought me too poor with the few possessions that I spoke of, he did not say as much.

When he had finished writing upon the paper he gave it to me and told me I must get my husband to sign it in front of the men. So I caught the tram back to Botany and saw to Charles, who had not improved while I was out. I put the piece of paper aside for some time to tend to him, for he was in the way of needing some cleaning – although I shall not go into details about that, sir – for though the children had sat with him and kept him good company, they had not looked after him as a wife might. Once I had tidied Charles and made him comfortable, he asked me how I had got on at the life insurance people, and I said they had told me he should sign a will if he thought himself that unwell. As I said it, I realised I had not mentioned the bed on which Charles lay, which was a fold-out stretcher type that we had placed in the sitting room so that he may look out the window easier. But I suppose the stretcher was not worth much.

Charles said that he would like to see the will then, and I said there was no hurry, for he would soon be well and Charles said he would like to see the will anyway and there was no time like the present and so I fetched it.

He read through the will and said I should have it witnessed then and there and that I should go next door and see if any of the men were home for he would read it aloud and sign it now.

And so it was at his urging that I went to find some men to sign his will and saw Mrs Collis and asked if the men were at home, for I needed them. So those who said that I was urging for the will to be signed, well, I was, but I was urging on Charles's behalf, you see.

When the men came into the sitting room to sign the documents, Charles was lying upon the settle, for he was not always in the fold-out bed when he was sick, as it often needed airing, you will understand.

Charles read his will aloud and then he signed it, and the men put their signatures on the page also.

And then the men left.

Charles got sicker and sicker. And on his last morning, his voice was very weak.

He said he wanted to tell me something, and I said he should save his strength, for by that time it seemed to take him a great effort to speak. And he spoke of his own father dying and the sadness this had caused him, and I knew then how low Charles had become, for he had not ever spoken at length of this incident since we were first married and I had asked after his family. He did not like to speak of it, but on this occasion he told me the story of how his father had been so low that he had tried to take his own life, and then fallen into even greater despair when he was unsuccessful at this. So his father had tried again and again and eventually he succeeded. And that this story was reported in the papers. To hear the details, oh my, sir, they sounded so sorrowful, and here was my husband, fighting to keep his life, and telling me how his father had taken his own.

And Charles sobbed as he spoke of this.

Now, we had lost two children and had many heartbreaks and disappointments of our own, but I had never seen my husband cry in this way, and I think it was because he himself was ill, and it was the talking of his father's death, which happened so long ago, that brought him to such sad tears.

I think it was the shame of it, sir.

It was as though in those last few days he had on Earth, when Charles thought himself to be dying, he wanted to clear his conscience. I held his hand and said he had played no part in his father's actions and had no guilt to bear. And I said his own father had no guilt for taking his life, for if what Charles said was how it had occurred, then his father was not well at the time and could not be blamed. I told Charles that he had always been the best of fathers to his own children. And we both cried. But it was true enough, for he was always a very good father to his children.

When we had finished a little weep, he said it was nice for us to be together and I said it was.

And he thanked me for nursing him, and I said nothing, for I felt the tears coming just at that time, and I did not want to upset him by my crying, for as I have said, I am not normally a woman given to weeping and so I smiled and patted his hand.

Then he slept for a time.

When he woke, he was troubled and I said, What is it, my dear – as I had been calling him dear while he was so unwell – and I was thinking he was fretting over his father again, so I told him not to worry about this as he had done no wrong. He said it was not that, it was something else, and by this time his voice was barely more than a whisper. But he said he wanted to tell me something, another thing he worried upon.

It was then he told me, sir, just at that moment, as we were sharing an intimacy, well, he told me that he had a wife previous and a child.

At first I said to him that I had heard something of these rumours when we had married in Merriwa and I reminded him I had asked him at the time and he had said it was gossip, because I was thinking, sir, that he was worrying over a past argument between us, one we had many years before.

And here he whispered yes, and I thought he was saying he remembered our discussing this gossip, but then he said, But she died and then the child, and before he could say more a pain gripped him.

Now, you may understand the effect this had on me. I had been in this marriage for over twenty years and was only now hearing of this life my husband had before he met me, which we had discussed when I first heard the rumour as a new bride, and I was thinking how he had not shared this story with me in all those years.

When his pain eased a little, I asked him had they been married before the law or just as a common man and wife, and he looked at me blankly and whispered, Who was married? and seemed to have forgotten what it was he had said. He was like that near the end. Just at that moment, a neighbour came to visit and Charles did not seem to recognise him, and I thought Charles's mind was wandering and that his talk of the marriage and someone dying was just a confusion.

But I worried all the same, as I had heard that gossip many years before. I did not know what I should do about him saying he had been married before me, or if it was even true, for he was badly affected by his illness at that time. I did not want to trouble him, but I also thought if Charles died then I would never find the truth of the matter. And I thought, If he has been married before, then perhaps he is still married to that woman, and when I stood up with him in the church all those years ago, perhaps it meant nothing. For he had not told me if she died before or after we were married, and so I was not sure.

And what of the child? But then I thought, what of any of it, because he was confused, as I said – he was so very ill and his mind was wandering. And I was sure he had said he was a bachelor on our marriage certificate, and he would have said he was a widower, wouldn't he?

I thought a great deal on all these matters, sir, as I am sure you will understand, and even though my husband was so sick, and I was caring for him, these things worried me.

But I was never able to ask him.

Charles died later that afternoon.

44.

I was with him at the end, and he slipped so ill with his sickness that it became hard to tell if he was still breathing. When he had gone, I closed his eyes, for he had asked me to do this, and I left him lying just as he was.

Then I brought in the children, for I had sent the little ones out to play in the street so Charles might have his rest, and I took them in to kiss their father goodbye. And then I sent May for Mrs Law as I needed to go see the money people and to fetch Mrs Price to arrange the body. Mrs Price was the one who did such body washing in Botany and so I went to get her and see the bank and then the insurance people.

One of the neighbours came in and I told them Charles had died, but that I needed to go out, on account of how much there was to be done, and I was in a very great distraction thinking of these things.

Charles being ill had placed us behind in the rent, and we did not have very much food in the house, plus there were the expenses of the doctors, and so, yes, when he died I did first think of money. But you must remember this, sir, Charles had been telling me he was dying since he first became unwell, so by the time it actually happened I was prepared. In shock, all the same, but I had been sitting there and going over in my mind the list of things which needed to be done.

I had written out a list of what Charles had told me to do if he died, for early on in his illness he was convinced that he would, and this was a list of the things Charles wanted me to do, but written in my hand.

That piece of paper is long gone. We had a little book where we would keep a record of our boarders paying their rent and Charles would write in it with a small pencil, and the list was written upon a page of this book, and I know I threw out the book later, after Charles had died.

It was Charles himself who said the things I must do – go to the insurance people and the like – and so when he died I was in need of doing all these things on the list, according to my husband's instructions. A visit to the doctor was first on the list, for Charles had said a death certificate would need to be completed before the insurance money would be paid.

And it was said that I behaved very odd after Charles died and did not act as a mourning widow should and seemed very distracted. But I cannot remember what I did, on account of me thinking how Charles had died and that I needed to do a great many things, as he himself had told me. And even if I did behave strangely, I do not see that this makes a person a murderer. The lawyer was trying to show that I was not grieving enough, but when have they had a husband die and a list of things they needed to do?

It is only the rich folk who can afford a whole change of clothes when there is a death, and there are not so many deaths among the rich as there are among the poor. I had a plain black bonnet and I bought a simple set of mourning buttons and placed them upon my mauve-grey gown and they sit there still, if they had cared to have a look upon it.

But when I was on the tram, and doing the jobs written on the list, what I kept thinking, sir, over and over, was that I had married Charles when I was very young and did not really want to, and I had given up my life with the Missus in her pretty home. I had stopped being Louisa and become Mrs Andrews just as my parents had asked me to. I had so long been Mrs Andrews that I had forgotten who Louisa was. And what I was thinking was that there may have been another Mrs Andrews before me, and in any case my husband was dead and now I would not ever know.

And I had so much grief and confusion, so I hardly knew who I was at all.

Law Report
SUPREME COURT
IN BANCO.—(BEFORE THEIR HONORS THE CHIEF JUSTICE, MR. JUSTICE WINDEYER, AND MR. JUSTICE FOSTER.)
REGINA V. LOUISA COLLINS

Mr. Rogers, Q.C., and Mr. Lusk, instructed by Messrs. Slattery and Heydon, appeared for the prisoner, and moved for a writ of error to quash the conviction of Louisa Collins, who was found guilty at the last Criminal Assizes of the murder of her husband, and sentenced to death. The grounds submitted were—1. That all the evidence which was admitted relative to the death of Charles Andrews was improperly admitted. 2. That one of the jurymen received and read a telegram, the contents of which were not known to the presiding Judge ...

Application refused and conviction confirmed.

The Sydney Morning Herald[18]

45.

The court has rejected my appeal.

Mr Lusk says the court looked at two reasons to excuse my being found guilty of murdering Michael. He says the court decided that neither of these things meant I had been tried unfairly.

I tell him I do not understand.

I ask when he might appeal again.

He looks down at one of his hands, turns it over to see the palm, and then he says the court will not allow another appeal.

I ask if May's testimony was discussed.

He shakes his head.

I tell him the things they looked at in the appeal were not the right things to consider, but May changing her story might convince them as they had listened so closely to her words.

He says he will not be able to appeal again. Then he says the judges who heard the appeal were the ones who had already ruled over the trials and so were most familiar with the circumstances.

I ask him if he is sure he cannot appeal again.

He does not answer my question but says I should have hopes of a reprieve and that I should appeal to my friends in parliament.

So I tell him I have none, as I am a woman, and I may not even vote.

46.
―――――――

Today they come to cut my hair.

They say I must have short hair for them to hang me, although I do not know why. Perhaps so the phrenologist who sat in court can feel my skull properly when I am dead, and tell them what sort of evil I was.

Maybe he shall make a death mask.

The barber comes into my cell with two of the warders, Anderson and Bryce. Alice is already in my cell and she stays.

I think the barber is practised in cutting men's hair. He gives me an ugly cut. Perhaps I just think this as it is so short.

I have no mirror, but Warder Anderson says it is quite fetching and some women are opting to have their hair cut in a short style and she is sure one day it will be that many women will choose to have their hair cut this way, for it is very practical. Alice says it is practical but not very pretty.

Then she says that I should not worry though, for my hair will soon grow and then she pauses and holds a horrified look. I laugh at the look upon her face, and I say I look forward to its being long again.

Later, Alice pats me on the hand and says they may not hang a woman, for all that they say that they will, for there have been three juries who have not been able to convict me, and only one which has found me guilty.

But I see the other warders share a look between themselves.

The barber is collecting locks of my hair from the floor, mementoes, I think, of the Botany Bay Murderess.

So I bend over and pick up some of the locks myself, and I give some of these to Alice and the other warders.

For it is my hair and I shall give the locks to whomever I please.

47.

May visits me today and I keep my cap on so that she will not see my short hair.

We try to be happy as this may be our last time together, but she is very distressed at seeing me. It is not good for a child to see their mother in a place such as this, with the warders and May's guardian in the room staring at us; it is all very crowded and formal.

May lies with me on the bed and I hold her to my chest and I stroke her hair, for this is something she has always enjoyed. We speak of happier times: when we were dancing together last year, the visits we had made to the beach at Botany, and of our old horse King. Even though May was very young when Charles sold King, and does not have many memories of her own, we have often spoken of him, and speaking of this horse makes her happy.

I try not to talk of her father, so as not to upset her, so I tell her of the lady I used to work for who loved to grow flowers, and of Blackie, and the boy named Harry who gave me a ribbon with bluebirds embroidered on it and she lies very still and clings to me, and listens.

Then we share a little sleep together and when I wake she is still holding me but she is asleep. And I look upon my child and I cannot believe that the government would kill me and take me from her. They must grant me a reprieve.

The whole time May and I are together, Alice has turned herself so she is not watching me directly and even the guardian has faced the other way, so that May and I might feel as though it were only us in the room. It is a kindness although it does not help much.

When May wakes I tell her that I have written a letter in which I said I would let her go and live with another family, for she cannot live with me here in the gaol. I tell her that she must not think I have done this because I do not love her, but that it was because this other family were very sad, and had no children. And that they particularly wanted a little girl called May to come and live with them and make them happy. I say I hope she might still be able to visit me. And I give her a lock of my hair as a remembrance, and I kiss her cheek and say she needs to go now for it will soon be getting dark, and I motion for Alice to call the guard to open the door.

I tell her I might see her again soon.

The door to the cell opens and I hold May a little longer and then I tell her that one day a dear friend might come to see her and bring a message from me to her, and this will not happen until my little May is a grown-up lady. Even though this might seem to be a long way in the future, May should always remember that a message from her mother will be coming.

I say that I love her.

The guardian nods to me, and she herself has tears on her cheeks and then she takes May by the hand and I watch them leave together and the door shut.

The Female Governor has the letter which gives the care of my little May over to another family who will have her now, whether I hang or not, and I will not be able to ever get her back.

48.

The chaplain comes to my cell tonight. I think he might have been summoned by a warder.

I roll over to face the wall.

He sits upon the edge of my bed and he rubs me lightly on my shoulder. He does not speak.

Neither do I.

It is most improper, but what is proper in all of this?

49.

I may have less than a week to live.

So when I wake today I determine that I should see Canon Rich this morning, and I ask Warder Bryce to arrange this for me.

She escorts me over to the Chapel with Warder Armstrong, and when I am seated at the table, Warder Armstrong leaves the room.

The chaplain comes in and says, Louisa, I am pleased to see you are feeling a little better.

There is my own name again, I think.

I say, I am, sir, on account that I would like to write some letters.

He says he will get me pen and ink and paper and asks that I might be unshackled, just at the wrists, so that I might write my letters freely.

I am going to write to each of my children, I say. I shall leave these letters for the authorities to give to my children should I not be reprieved.

The chaplain looks to Warder Bryce, who does not hesitate,

and she does not seek the permission of the Female Governor either; she simply undoes the handcuffs and sets my hands free.

I thank her and when the stationery comes, I begin to write.

Canon Rich begs his pardon to be excused to go up into the Chapel, and that this will give me some privacy to tend my letters.

In each letter, I will tell my children of my love for them, and the love their father had for them.

I try to say one happy story for each of them – a story from our trip to Sydney upon the dray, when Charles set a campfire each night and it was like a holiday; or our times at the bay in Botany or out the back with the boarders. I write a memory of a happy time with their parents for each of them and before long a large stack of envelopes sit beside me. I do not seal any of these, as they will be read by others before the children may have them.

I check to see if Warder Bryce is looking and she is not; she is dozing, her head tipped forward.

And so I write one more letter. An extra one, just for May. One which I will give to my friend for safekeeping until May becomes of age. I want to say things to May which you cannot say to a child, and which will need to wait until she is a grown woman. I have thought upon the words carefully and so I am able to write quickly and then I seal this letter and place it inside my sleeve. The letter will only matter if they hang me, and if they do, May must know she was but a child in a world of men who used their power to find me guilty. She must not carry any burden upon herself.

I tell her she is the innocent in all of this.

And I explain why.

Then I lay the pen down and push the ink bottle forward slightly. The stack of letters will be taken to the Prison Governor, and he shall read every one before he permits them to be given out, as is required for prisoners' letters. I know this because he has done this with all my letters before.

Then I sit quietly and wait for someone to tend me. For Warder Bryce to wake up, for Warder Anderson to come back, or for Canon Rich to finish in the Chapel.

In spite of myself, I smile at how well guarded I am.

50.

Charles was buried at Rookwood cemetery, sir, and I chose a plot with a view of the bush, which I thought would be peaceful for him to have his rest. I do not like to think upon this now as he has been so disturbed, being dug up for the inquest.

Many people came to see Charles off from our house, for he was well liked and respected.

Michael came to the funeral and was a very great comfort to me, as though I may not have shown it to the satisfaction of those around me, I was greatly distressed. Charles had been my husband for over twenty years and now he was no more, and though we had not been happy, I felt his loss just the same.

I also knew that my life had changed, sir, as I no longer had a man to care for me.

I had not seen Michael during the time when Charles was sick, because Michael knew Charles had developed a great dislike for him, and he did not want to upset Charles further by visiting.

I wanted to hold a wake for Charles and at the time I had the coin for this on account of the insurance money coming to me.

Michael helped me with the arrangements.

We arranged beer from the hotel and Michael and I visited Mr Sayers, the grocer at the end of the road, as he knew Charles very well and he came to know Michael well also. In fact, I would say they became great friends. We asked Mr Sayers to provide a selection of cakes and treats and some sugar drink. And we asked one of the workers Charles had known when he was working at Geddes, a fellmonger who had a way with music, to come and play upon his tin whistle.

So we set up the table and some chairs and Mr Sayers came down and laid the table with treats — cakes with coloured icing, sandwiches and sweets — and all the neighbours came and everyone helped themselves to the food and drink, and there was dancing. The party went on until one or two in the morning.

May came over to me and then, as the tin whistle was played, she and I linked hands and we danced twirling around the room and she was laughing and her hair was swinging back and she looked so happy and pretty.

I remember thinking to myself at the time that I used to have hair like that, and that I was only a little older than May when young Harry had brought me the hair ribbon and how that girl I had been seemed a world away. And I thought I was glad I had money and I could buy May some hair ribbons and make her hair pretty.

I do not want to think of my May as she looked upon me when she gave her story in the court, for each time it was a knife in my heart.

No sir, I think of her as she was on that day, at the wake we had for Charles, when she held my hands and I spun her around the room and her hair flicked back and then later when she was laughing with a cake in her hand and pink icing upon her cheeks.

That is how I think of my May.

51.

And it was a few days after the wake that Michael came to board.

Now, there are those who say it was not the right thing to do, but then there will always be those, won't there, sir, and I was a widow alone with many small children and I was in need of comfort and company.

Michael had been living back at my house for a few weeks when he went to Sydney upon the tram. This was not unusual for him to do, sir, but on that day, he came home not long after he had left, with a bunch of roses and some nice cheese, and he sent May to the hotel for some beer, for he said I was in need of some cheering.

I placed the roses on the table, having put them in a jug which we used to hold water, as I had no vase.

And I said to him that he must have bought them from the market in Sydney, as there was no flower seller in Botany, and how nice it was that he had thought to get me roses. He said he had done this as I had told him of the Missus and her roses and I said that was good of him to remember.

And Michael and I sat and talked and drank the beer and ate the cheese and he asked me what my plans were, and would I open a boarding house as some widows do, and I said I did not need to as I had money now. He asked me how much money as, he said, he might help me set up a business of some sort, for I would need a man in the front of such a plan even though I were a respectable widow, and did I have a business in mind.

I said I did not, except that I knew I did not want to have another butcher shop, and we laughed a little at that, for I had told him how unhappy I was when I was working in the shop. I said there would come a time when I would need to think about work, but that time was a long way off yet and that I did not wish to think of such things.

He sat for a good while and stared at the bottom of his glass and then he said that he should like to help me with my future plans, but the uncertainty of his gambling wins was more suitable for a single man, and he would not like to have a wife and children in such a life, for the money ebbed and flowed.

Then he said that he was ashamed to ask, particularly as it was so soon after the passing of my first husband, but he said he should like to marry me, except he felt he had so little to offer a woman of my calibre.

I was taken aback. He had seen me washing and cleaning and cooking for boarders, and I said so, and he told me that part of my charm was that I was prepared to do anything to feed my children and honour my wedding vows. At the mention of my wedding vows, I did not tell Michael what Charles had said upon his death bed about being married previous.

I simply said I would always work to make do.

And at that point he placed down his glass and he asked me if I might marry him, and it was a proposal in the way that every woman dreams a marriage proposal would be, for there were flowers in the room, and we had our drinks and our cheese, and so I said yes.

I am sure Michael loved me, as I know Charles did, in his own way.

In April we were married at the church near Waterloo station.

And I wanted to tell you, sir, my story of how Michael asked me to marry him and how he loved me, and I him.

52.

On one of the first Saturdays after our marriage, Michael caught the tram and went to the Randwick races, for he said that he knew of another bookie who might take him on for work. I had said that I would like to come with him, as I wanted to go wherever he might go.

But Michael said that women such as me would not go to the races for he said some of the women there were of questionable standards, and so I didn't go, but I gave him some money to bet.

He did not have much luck betting on the horses that day, or finding the bookie that he might work for. When he came home he told me that he had lost the pound which he had taken, saying it was the fault of the bookies, for the only one he had ever felt to be honest was the one he had worked for who had now gone to Queensland.

Michael's mentioning Queensland again alarmed me, for even though he was married he might still go, for many a man went elsewhere and left his wife while he did. So I told him that there was no need to be worried about the money for there was much more to be had and that Charles had left me well provided for.

I gave him another pound, to make up for his losses at the races.

And to take his mind from Queensland, I said that I thought we should travel to Ballarat to meet his family, as he had often talked of the place where he grew up. He said that we should do this, for there would come a time when he might be the one managing a large property, if his father saw fit to give him the responsibility.

The next day he mentioned going to Victoria again as he and I strolled out on the Sunday afternoon, and stopped in at the hotel. I had said I would have liked to use my parasol – for I had one from my wedding – and Michael said the parasol was too grand for the likes of this particular hotel and that the next week he would take me to the Sir Joseph Banks Hotel, where we might stroll through the gardens and see the menagerie. He told me I might use my parasol there, for it would not be out of place, and that May could take care of young Charlie as she was quite old enough. And he said I should be sure to bring my parasol when we went to Ballarat, for there were fine gardens and all the ladies strolled with a parasol. I said I had heard tell Ballarat was a fine gold area, and he said that the country around it was worth far more than gold for all the sheep it could grow.

I talked with him of some of the properties on which we lived and how I had not seen my mother for many years, since we moved to Sydney, and so there were several of the children who she had not even met, although we exchanged frequent letters. I said that it saddened me that my father had died since I moved to Sydney and I had not been able to go to the funeral, on account of the letter not reaching me in time.

So I asked him if he might think of moving up to the country, to be near my mother. And he asked if it had been my brother who inherited the family property when my father died and I laughed that he would think such a thing. He said that he thought I had been from a well-to-do family.

Now, sir, never in my life had I heard such a thing thought of me. I liked my drink and to sing and dance. I told him my father had only worked upon the different properties and we did not ever own them.

Michael was silent a moment and then began to describe his own family's property. He spoke of a sweeping drive and a two-storey homestead and the paddock which flowed down to the river. He said the fences were in a state of disrepair, but there were strong solid gums which grew along the river banks and he would soon have good fence posts from them, and he spoke of how the wheat would dip and wave when the heads were full and the wind blew.

I asked how he could ever have left such a beautiful place, and he said he had very grand plans for when he came into ownership and he would extend the thousand acres by purchasing the neighbouring farms, and increase the land under wheat.

He spoke as though he missed the property, and so I said I would like to see it. And then he grew quiet and I said, What is wrong, my love? and he said, Louie, I feel that I may have cursed my father now, for I have spoken of when he is gone, and I worry I might not see him again. I think speaking about my own father being dead may have added to his worry, sir. So I said that of course he should go to see his father and then he said that he did not think I should travel with him, at least at first, but that I should let him tell his family of his marriage before they met me. And I said had he not written to them and told them of our marriage, and he said he had not.

I did not rightly understand this, how he could marry but not tell his family. But later, I came to think that his family was not on such a large property as Michael described, for by then I had begun to wonder if many of his stories were added to and played up to sound bigger. And even though I loved him, I did not know quite what to believe sometimes.

53.

A month or so after our wedding, Michael and I moved to Johnson's Lane, for Michael had expressed an interest in living in that part of Botany, it being a better area of town. And so we rented a cottage there, although the rent was dearer than we paid in Frog's Hollow. I bought myself a few nice things, a tea set and a vase, and these reminded me of all the pretty things I had dusted for the Missus.

And it was then that our son, William John, was born, but I shall come to that sad story directly.

But we were not as happy in Johnson's Lane as we had expected to be. The Sir Joseph Banks Hotel and Pleasure Gardens was very grand, but it was an expensive place to be regularly drinking. Also, it was frequented by different folk from those we were used to seeing, and so after just a few months we decided to move back to Frog's Hollow. I sold some of my new dresses and the tea set and the vase and then my parasol – as Michael said this was all too grand for us now – and he sold one of his new suits.

The money from the insurance people, which had seemed such a large sum, well, it was disappearing. I had paid off my own debts and Michael's as well, and he was not working so we had no money coming in, but there was still plenty going out on rent and food and the like. When we came back to Pople's Terrace, I was clear of debt and still had some twenty-five pounds in gold, which was a lot of money, but nothing compared to what I had received when Charles died. And so we made economies.

Michael found work at one of the fellmongers but he was only there about six weeks before he lost his position. He said he thought his boss had taken a dislike to him.

But after he had lost that job, he was then several weeks without work and did not appear to be able to find employment, even though he was a fit young man. I should say, though, work was hard to find at the time, as there were fluctuations in the need for labour, and even my own boys, who were good workers like their father, well, even they had to travel to find work.

Michael said to me that he thought he would go and make some money at a gambling house which he had been to in the past, one which is on George Street. I now know that gambling establishments are not fair in their business and do not have a care if they take more money from people than people can afford, but I did not know that then.

I did not like the thought of him going there for I have heard there is a certain kind of woman who frequents those places, although you would probably not know of this, sir, as you will have never been, and neither have I, of course, but I have heard stories.

Now, all this was in my statement, the one I said in the inquest court, the same one which has been read out at each of my trials since, so you do not need to hear it again.

The chaplain says he would like me to tell him anyway.

Well, that Saturday night, he borrowed a pound from me and he went off to the gamble game.

He came back very late, but he was pleased, because he had turned that one pound into more than four. Four pounds and ten shillings. He told me the money was easier to make there than when he went to work carting the green skins or working in the other factories, that he could make more money in a shorter time.

He said to me that if he had twenty pounds that night, he would have been able to make one hundred pounds, and that it would have been easily done, and that by such a venture, only once or twice a year, we should be able to live a fine life. He said again that he wished I had given him more money for that very evening, as Lady Luck was on his side, but he was sure that she would favour him again next time he visited.

But I was not convinced that gambling was a good idea, even though Michael had just brought me over four pounds. Charles had not been a gambler and so I was only just becoming accustomed to having a husband who gambled.

Then he said, You have twenty pounds, don't you, Louie?

I said he knew I did, for we did not have secrets in this regard.

And he said that if I gave him my twenty pounds to use on the next Saturday he would bring me back one hundred in return, for it was a sure thing that he would win again. It was just like a business venture, he said. An investment, he called it.

I told him that this would be my last twenty pounds, and I did not think he should gamble with so much money. And I told him I was glad to see the four pounds he had made, but that we should go to sleep for it was late.

Through that week he was out looking for work and found none, and he had only had a few days' work in the last month or so. And he would ask me about the money and say again he was sure he could make my twenty pounds into one hundred and I should give it to him. And, well, sir, I suppose by the time the

Saturday came around, he had convinced me and so I gave him my twenty pounds and he went back into Sydney, I think to the same house on George Street.

He did not come home with money.

He had lost everything.

I said, What do you mean? Lost it all, what do you mean? And I asked where my hundred pounds was. And he looked at me and shook his head and then I myself began to cry.

He had not made me one hundred pounds, and he had lost all of the twenty besides.

I could say nothing, sir. All that money. Gone.

I still feel sick even now thinking of it, for we had nothing, nothing, and me with all the children.

And I think I said that he had promised me, or something like, for I was very upset.

He asked me to forgive him.

When I saw his sad state, and the misery on his face, I said I would have to, sir, which in truth was the case, for there was no getting the money back. And he spoke of the gambling house and how wrong it was that they would take such an amount of money from people who had none, and that places like that should not be allowed to do such things.

We spent a restless night of worry.

Michael had a cup of tea the next morning when we rose, and we sat and talked of the money again and of how we could get it back and then of where he might go to look for work. We sat for a considerable time talking over this, sir, and he said he thought that he might catch the train and try for some work away from Botany, up the Illawarra line, for he had heard there was work at some factories there and he asked me to give him money for the fare.

I gave him a pound, on account of his saying if he found any work he would take it and so he would be away for the whole week and would need to board.

And I think it was the next day that he left.

He came back that night and, well, I was surprised, sir, and when I asked him why he had come home, could he find no work, he said nothing at first, but after I persisted asking, he told me the story.

He said he caught the train from the city, but had bought the wrong ticket and gone out several miles further on the train than his ticket had allowed, for he was not familiar with that train line, and did not know the stations.

When he went to get off at the station he said the guard had looked at his ticket and had seen that he had gone too far for what he had paid and was being rough with Michael, and they argued, with their fists I believe, sir.

Michael had to pawn his watch to pay a fine. Now, I had bought him that watch as a wedding present, and here we had even less money and he still had no work and now no watch besides. I told him that we would get the watch back, and he said, Louie, we are ruined.

He was very low when he said this, but I was angry, sir, for when Charles had died I had so much money and now it was gone and I was worried how we would pay the rent and eat, what with him out of work, and I thought we might end up on the street. And we had a row, sir, over the money. Well, it was not really a row – it was more just me being angry with him, for he was too low to bother arguing back. And he kept saying that he had failed us, and in the end I told him to stop saying this.

Michael got some work carting skins and he was earning thirty-six shillings per week. He was still very downhearted and so I said that if we put a little aside he might be able to redeem his watch but he said there would not ever be enough money and on any account he could not remember the place where he had pawned it.

I pressed him and said that surely if we went to the area he would remember where he had pawned it. And he said he never could, and so we did not speak ever of it again.

54.

After I gave birth to my son William John Collins, well, sir, I have never seen a father dote upon a baby as much as Michael did upon this child. We called him William on his birth certificate, but we used the name John for the baby.

John was a difficult baby; there are no two ways about it. He wanted to be held all the time and he had a bad colicky stomach, and he cried a lot. But none of this seemed to bother Michael, who would get up to him at night and bring him into our bed to soothe him. Michael was patience itself, and adored the baby, and he was a lovely blessing for us.

But you should be careful when counting your blessings, sir.

On the night my John died, Michael was holding him in his arms and the death of his son, well, it broke Michael's heart.

Now, I have known the death of a baby before, of course, but it is the type of death which you never really harden to, in the way you might harden to the death of older people. The death of a baby is not in the natural way of things, as they have done none of their living before their time comes to be dying, so the death of a baby seems extra hard.

For the mother, if your baby dies it is as though you lose a part of yourself and you hold the death of a baby close and think of it every new day, for, you tell yourself, today the baby would have been doing this or that or would have had a birthday. I used to think as it was only the mother who felt like this, but I know Michael felt John's death keenly, and where his birth had given him joy, the death brought him despair.

I think that the death of our son also brought a great sadness upon our marriage, for we were no longer the light and happy couple we had been, teasing and joking. Michael grieved so over the child and to watch this was very hard. He was too down in his own grief to comfort me, even though I had lost the child too, but I still had to put meals on the table and wash clothes. There were times I was glad for the distraction that being busy with these things gave me from thinking of my dead baby.

Michael did not want to go to work and lay upon the bed and he kept saying the child had not been long in the world, which was true enough, but to hear the way Michael said this, over and over in such a melancholy fashion, well, it was very sad indeed, sir.

I was glad that Michael was not there in the court to hear the way the doctors spoke about our child, for they talked of what they found when they dug up the little body – of the kidneys and the parts which had rotted away. It nearly broke my heart to hear them speak this way, talking about 'that' specimen. He wasn't just one of their science things sitting in a jar – he was my child, and all that was left of the little baby I birthed, who I had held in my arms and nurtured as a mother does, and loved. Those doctors should be ashamed to talk of my baby that way.

I had no money to pay for John's funeral so I had to borrow over one pound off Mrs Bullock.

I used this money to pay for the ground for our John to be buried. I have never yet been able to pay Mrs Bullock back, but she has not asked me for the money, which is very kind of her, and I have written to her from gaol to say that I shall pay her back just as soon as I am able. I still owe the doctor his fee for the visit for the death certificate as well.

Michael was no longer the happy rogue he had been when we first met. I tried to tell him that there might be more children, but he did not like me saying this, as he said no other child would replace John and in any case he did not want any more as he did not want to be put through the sadness of another baby dying.

He was working when John died, but he said to me that there was no point in working, for he would never make enough in wages to pay back our debts.

And he began to wake from his sleep and imagine that he heard John crying and he would look about for the baby. And at other times he said he heard someone outside or imagined them throwing berries upon the roof of the cottage and I asked him who this might be, and why would they do such a thing? He used to say, Can you hear them, Louie? and I confess, sir, I never heard this myself.

I have lately written of these berries to my mother, for there are some which grow in Botany and people say they will make you sick. Perhaps it was these which made my Michael sick, or he thought they made him so. I do not know, but we all lived in the same house, sir, and none of the rest of us were unwell.

I think it was the stress of losing our baby that caused him to worry so about money, and the bailiff and the like.

At one time I said he should try his hand at the gamble again, or at the races. He said that if I was to stop the drinking it might be easier to feed the children. I told him that there was a time when he had enjoyed coming for a drink and had been a much nicer man for it, which I think was not the right thing to be saying.

I tried to be kind, but there were times when I found him vexing. Although I know it is not right to say this of the dead, and it was only on a few occasions that I was annoyed, I am sure.

I was pleased when Michael returned to working, for it was good for him to be out of the house and doing something, and I did not have him being sad around me all day. But he told me fellmongering was not the sort of work which he wanted to do and that any man who had owned two suits should not have to do such low work as this. He thought it was beneath him, sir, was what he meant. And it well might have been, for it is filthy, dirty work, but my Charles had done such work and worse besides, killing beasts and the like. And there was that difference between them, you see. Charles just accepted this sort of work as his lot and got on with the doing of it.

I have wondered since I have been in gaol whether there ever was a farm waiting for Michael or whether he had only imagined there was, dreaming that he himself was destined for better things, much as I myself used to hope for a home like the one the Missus had.

And I think that perhaps Michael came to understand that this was just a fanciful dream when John died and he found he could not even pay for the coffin. When your dreams die, it is part of growing up and accepting your lot in life. That can be a hard lesson when it comes.

And it was around this time, while Michael was so low in spirits, that he became unwell, although, to start with, we both thought it was only a cold.

He had a few days' working on the cart which carried the green skins from Glebe Island and he would sit upon the bloodied skins as he rode on the cart.

And he did this on and off for about a fortnight, but he complained of a lump in his groin – although I never did see this myself, sir. There was also a sore upon his leg, a cut or graze, that he had for some time, and which would not heal.

I first noticed this when I saw him limping and, well, I could smell something upon him and it smelt like meat when it had gone bad, but when I asked him about it, he said to let him alone, that it was nothing and he had been to the chemist and been given a powder which he was taking.

He could not bear his leg to be exposed to the air and so he said that he would keep his trousers on in bed, if I was agreeable, for then the blanket would not irritate his leg.

Of course, I said, I was agreeable if it gave him comfort.

The next week I was preparing to do the wash and it must have been a Monday, for I always did the wash of a Monday. I was hanging his warm coat and brushing it to see if it needed a wash, and in the breast pocket I found a small package wrapped in paper, and when I opened it, there was some white powder inside. I thought this might be the medicine which Michael had spoken of.

So I asked him and he told me that it was and I asked what the medicine was called and he said he did not rightly know the name, but he had been recommended it by a friend.

And I said he would do better to have a poultice if he had a sore, for a poultice will draw the poison right out of a wound, if applied properly, sir. And he said he would rather use the learnings of the man he saw at Waterloo than the meddlings of an old woman, and so I did not say anything more, sir, as I did not like him speaking to me in this way.

But I do still think a poultice might have been best, as it could have been that sore on his leg which killed him.

Over the next few days, he continued to be going about his

business and heading to work, although his leg seemed to be causing him some pain. A few times I asked him if he wanted me to mix the powder for him, thinking I might help him and it might ease his discomfort, but he said he did not need me to mix anything for him, and so I did not and I did not see him use the powder either, though I did ask him several times if he was taking it.

He woke on the Saturday morning at four o'clock and he went off to work.

When he came home for his breakfast, he asked for some milksops and so I gave him a bowl and he put the bread and milk in himself and made them, but after only a little while I heard him in the yard, retching violently. I went out to tend to him and asked if it was the powder he was taking that was making him so sick and he said that he was not taking the powder at all and that it was the cold which was making him ill.

He went back to work, but I later heard a witness say Michael had needed to get down off the dray and be sick in the bushes. He came home and went to bed, but was very unwell all through that day and the next, and when he seemed no better, I took him to see the doctor in Elizabeth Street. We went on the tram, but the doctor would not see Michael or listen to his chest except if I paid for him to do it, and he made Michael come out to the waiting room to get the money from me, which must have been shameful for him to have to come and ask his wife for money in front of the doctor and other men who waited.

The doctor prescribed some medicine, a tonic and some powders and I got these from the chemist myself, or I sent one of the children to get them. Michael said that he was sure the medicine would do him no good but that he would take it anyway as otherwise it would be a waste of money going to the doctor. He said that he thought the bailiffs would come to the house soon, and so, with every knock upon the door, he became fearful that it would be them.

I told him that the only money I owed was to Mrs Bullock for our John, and that she would not be calling the bailiffs for she knew that I would pay my way in the end as I always did. Besides, I said, she would not be calling the bailiffs for a pound borrowed to bury a dead child.

When Michael's health did not improve I went in to see the doctor again myself and asked him to come out to see my husband, and he came back with me on the tram. And when he examined Michael he prescribed more powders.

They did not seem to make any difference, sir.

So the next day, or maybe the day after, I cannot be sure, I went back to the doctor and he came out, and he tried some new powders on Michael, and he also took some of Michael's vomit and fluids for testing.

But nothing seemed to help.

And there were more visits from the doctor and, oh, sir, there were so many medicines he was asking me to give to Michael. But I gave them all exactly as he said, and even with all the powders and tonics, Michael just got sicker and sicker; a young healthy man like that, it was a sorrow to watch.

And the doctor said I should take Michael to the hospital and I said I would do no such thing for all my life, for I told him it was known that all those who went to the hospital died there, and that hospitals were bad places. My thoughts on hospitals have not improved at all, sir, given what I know the doctors at the hospital did to my husband Charles and to my son John when they dug them up.

And when Michael was still so unwell, I sent one of the boys – Arthur, I think it was – up to Elizabeth Street on the tram to fetch the doctor out again and this was when the two doctors came to my house together. The doctor who I had been seeing to attend to Michael brought the one who had attended Charles; he wanted another opinion, I think, but I am not sure. Because there were so many doctor visits, and people coming and going in the house, and powders to be mixed, and each day of worry seemed to jumble in with the next.

All the while, Michael was bothered and worried that the bailiff might come, and he should not have been thinking of this, he should have been trying to get well.

Was there anyone who helped you while you nursed him, Louisa? the chaplain says.

I tell him that there was – the neighbours sat with me beside the bed, and Mrs Pettit stayed with me well into the night.

And did you have anyone pray with you, Louisa? he asks.

I did not, sir, I say. But I did try to get a priest for Michael, or at least the Sisters of Mercy, as he was Catholic, but there was none who could come.

Through his last night, Michael looked very bad, and his eyes had sunk back in his head. But he slept a little, sir, which was a kindness for him.

Now, sir, at some time in those last few days, Michael said to me, Louie, look to the lights here, and he pointed at something in the room, but I could not see anything there and so I said, There are no lights, my love.

And he said, No, Louie, there are so many stars all around, and green lights. There was one of our neighbours there with me, and they heard him say this as well.

When Michael breathed his last I was glad that he told me of the lights, for it made me think that he was going to a better place, and that his last thoughts were not of the bailiffs.

I quite lost my senses when Michael died. And I have been told since that I said I did not want to live without my Michael.

Much has been made of me saying this when Michael died and also some things I said when my husband Charles died as well, and the truth is, sir, I cannot rightly recall if I said these things or not. But what I said when Michael died has been taken to mean that I did not care for my own children, which of course was most upsetting to them, and is not true, as it was just my grief talking.

If I said things in grief, or if I mourned too little or too much for my husbands, that does not mean that I murdered them, sir.

55.

The constable came and took me from my home after Michael's death. We walked to the police station and I was tired and had been drinking and my heart was full of grief for my Michael.

There are those who think that I should not have remarried so soon after the death of my first husband, or that I should not have claimed the money from Charles's life insurance policy, but then they have not been a widow on their own, trying to raise children, and I have known other women who have had many more husbands besides, and not been charged with the killing of the earlier ones.

And they have branded me a murderess on the word of my own little daughter, and a nobbler glass they say was full of poison.

Yes, sir, I think I would like to pray with you now.

56.

For weeks I have been clinging to the thought that they will not hang a woman, but my appeal has failed and now the chaplain is telling me they may indeed hang me.

He says he knows people have been to see the Governor of New South Wales to beg for me.

And he says I should also write to him myself and beg for his mercy.

The chaplain says there is little time left to change the mind of those who will execute me.

I tell him that until that last step is taken, until the door opens and that last drop comes, until there is no breath in my body, there is still a chance those who can spare my life will do so.

I pray with the chaplain.

I pray to God for His mercy.

Then I write to the Governor.

And I beg for his as well.

57.

Darlinghurst Gaol, Sydney

7 January 1889

Some of the children come to visit me.
    We cry and cling.
    I cannot speak.

58.

Darlinghurst Gaol, Sydney

8 January 1889

They come to get me from my cell.

Alice has stayed with me through the night, and Warder Anderson came early this morning.

Both the warders shed tears as they each say their goodbyes to me, for we do this here instead of out upon the gallows.

I thank each of them in turn, and hold Alice for some time, although, I tell her, she will see me soon enough. I still have hopes of a reprieve.

I squeeze her hand. If I am not reprieved, she will keep my letter and give it to May when the child has grown older.

Canon Rich was here until late in the evening, and he has come back early this morning. We have spent the time praying for my soul, and I have prayed for a reprieve. I tell him what a great comfort he has been to me and that he is a good man.

I turn my hands out for the shackles and the Female Governor says we shall not need them today. She looks me in the face. I nod.

Then we all walk out together: the Female Governor, the many warders, the chaplain and myself.

Quite the parade.

Our procession walks from my cell to the end of the cell block and then out into the gaol yard.

This is the first time in a month I have been allowed to walk outside my cell without shackles.

I feel light.

All the prisoners are still locked in their cells as the governors do this when there is an execution. It is hot and the slop buckets shall be overflowing and the cells shall smell none too sweet.

We walk around the edge of the cell block and along past the Chapel, then we turn to the left and walk towards the men's largest cell block. I have never been to this part of the gaol. It is off limits to the women prisoners. I should like to have a care to look around me, but there is no time this morning.

I do take the time as we walk to look up at the sky. For one moment, I pause and tip my head back and look at the blue above me. My father would like this sky, and say it was a good omen.

I think, This is the same bright blue which covers my children and perhaps they look up as I do. I send my love to them upon this sky, and I pray that whenever the sky is blue, they may think of me.

Alice touches my elbow and gives me a gentle smile. We walk on.

We enter the large cell block and I think we go to another cell.

My arms are pinned in restraints.

I am not sure of time.

We mount the steps to the second floor.

I am walking upon the steps which may lead to my death.

I am still hopeful I shall be granted a reprieve.

They will never hang a woman.

Suddenly, we are at the scaffold, and I look down. There are a dozen men who wait patiently to see the entertainment I will provide.

I hear noise from outside the prison walls. I think a crowd has gathered.

I lose some of my nerve – there is little time left, perhaps there shall be no reprieve.

A hood is placed upon my face, and I cannot see those around me, though I hear quite clearly the voice of the chaplain as he prays beside me, the hawkers calling out across the wall that they sell locks of my hair. I hear Flora calling out, Hello, dearie, and I smile, in spite of myself.

I am glad for the hood which covers my face, for what should they think of a woman smiling as she is about to be hung?

The noose comes around my neck.

And then it is just Canon Rich I hear, and he is telling me to make my peace with God and not to be afraid. I hear a quivering in his voice.

He is a good, kind man.

I want to tell him that I am not afraid, because I shall yet be reprieved from this hanging, and given leave to live in the gaol. That the men who have brought my life to this point will suddenly realise the decisions they have made, and will call off this hanging. That at the last minute, the trapdoor will not open, and the Governor shall tell the hangman to lift the noose from my neck, and take the hood from my face.

I want to comfort the chaplain and tell him that all will be well, that I shall live in the gaol and my hair will grow long.

But I cannot speak.

Under the hood, I close my eyes, and I see all those who are around me.

I see my husbands, I see my boys, and I see May, as she was on the night that we held a wake for Charles.

I see her coming to me and skipping to the music, and I feel her take my hands as we dance.

Her hair is swinging out behind her and she has a blue ribbon around her curls, a ribbon embroidered with bluebirds.

She shall grow into a beauty.

I hope she may have her own life, not one thrust on her by others.

As I stand upon the scaffold, I hear them push the lever.

The trapdoor does not open.

———————

I am reprieved.

Epilogue

Darlinghurst Gaol, Sydney

8 January 1889

Today was a most heartbreaking scene. This morning I walked with the prisoner Mrs Collins, Louisa, as she went to her death.

We had spent much of the night in her cell, with warders in attendance. Warder Harper has been a calm companion and has served Louisa well.

Alice Harper was much affected.

Louisa continued until the very last to hold her stoicism that the government would not hang her.

Even yesterday she wrote a heartfelt plea to the Governor of New South Wales that he may yet spare her life, as he was in power to do.

Though she had no reply, Louisa continued to believe, even today, that she may be spared.

In the days before the execution, she would not have been able to see the scaffold but I have heard the banging of hammer into wood and the dull thud of the sandbags as they sampled the weight to ensure the correct drop length. I heard the hangman boasted he took extra care because he was hanging a woman, and was not in the way of killing them.

He still bungled the doing.

I went to Louisa early this morning and we prayed together. She spent her last hours in prayer and farewell, and though others were moved to tears, she was not. She walked boldly to the cell block which held the gallows. I have seen brutish men who have not held the same strength before death.

She did not stumble even when mounting the scaffold steps.

She stood on the scaffold in her rough prison dress, the hood over her head and the noose around her neck. She looked pitiful.

The trapdoor did not open at first, and I held my eyes upon Louisa. I saw a quiver run through her. She was determined that she should rely on a reprieve until the last breath left her body.

I knew when the door did not open immediately that this might give her some hope that she had been spared. I can only pray that this poor woman did not suffer too much in her last few anxious moments. I kept my voice low and constant, and prayed the Lord's Prayer for her, even as the hangman shouted for his assistant to *Pull, pull.*

I prayed and thought surely God would intervene in her ending and permit her to hear my voice?

I have no way of knowing if He did.

The hangman, fool that he is, stepped onto the platform and tried to see why the trapdoor was not working and then indicated to his assistant that he should knock the pin out from below.

A mallet was used by one of the warders and with each devastating blow I saw Mrs Collins tremble anew. But even as the number of blows grew, still the peg did not move and even I began to believe that her death may be reprieved, for surely the State would not be so cruel as to allow this torture to continue.

When her fall finally came, Louisa fell through the trapdoor with considerable force.

I hope the sharpness of her fall meant that her death was instantaneous, for once the door opened there was a gush of bright blood which squirted from just under the neck and blood sprayed everywhere and within a moment the body hung prostrate.

Through the gap made by the trapdoor, I could see the hood and its contents suspended at an acute angle, and the head appeared to be connected to the body by only a small stretch of sinew.

I wanted to close my eyes from the horror, but I kept them open for Louisa.

I kept praying.

Those who had thought to jeer her at her last were now quiet and shocked at the raw brutality of what they saw. The flies swarmed thicker and thicker, until they covered the gash at the neck and you could hear their drone throb as the body hung for the required twenty minutes.

There had been the intention for the burial to take place immediately, but because the hanging had been so badly done, there shall be some sort of enquiry as to how this came to be such a botched execution.

A coroner's jury may come and see the body as it lies in the prison morgue.

The phrenologist may feel her head, and determine through his science whether she was indeed a murderess.

---

9 January 1889

I went with Louisa's coffin on the cart and train which took her to Rookwood cemetery. She is not to be buried within the walls of the Darlinghurst Gaol, as is the custom for those who are executed. She shall have consecrated ground.

Several police and Warders Anderson and Harper came with me, although Alice did not come in her uniform.

Alice brought three pink roses, and when the prayers had been said and the coffin covered over, she placed these upon the grave.

Behind the Bars
In the Shadow of the Scaffold
By 'Ex-warder'

Louisa Collins was another specimen of the hoping condemned. 'They will never hang a woman,' she declared; 'they will spare my life at the last moment.' Then, when she saw it was all over ... she faintly said: 'And it has come to this?'

'If you have a confession to make,' urged the chaplain, 'do so now, as you have only a few minutes to live.'

'My confession will be made to God, before whom I shall appear to day,' she firmly answered.

The Arrow[19]

Author's Note

The Killing of Louisa is a work of fiction based on a true event. The real Louisa Collins was hung at Darlinghurst Gaol, Sydney, Australia, on 8 January 1889 after being tried four times for the murder of one or the other of her two husbands.

This novel is perhaps another layer of that story, one that could possibly fit parts of the record, one that I hope causes no offence to any living relative of the historical figures on which some of the characters are based. I have imagined interactions and conversations, trying not to stray too far from known or reported events, but straying nonetheless. I have fictionalised the historical figure of Canon Rich, but the content of some of the conversations between this character and the fictional Louisa are based on court documents and newspaper articles.

I was intrigued by the court cases themselves, and also by the many newspaper articles, pamphlets and public meetings; the discussions in parliament; the petitions and the passionate public debate that surrounded her trials. The real Louisa Collins was indeed executed in a dreadfully botched hanging where the trapdoor did not immediately open. The pin had to be bashed out with a mallet.

Acknowledgements

I am indebted to contemporary newspapers and archive material. The true crime books Caroline Overington's *Last Woman Hanged* and Carol Baxter's *Black Widow* were invaluable resources and their extensive annotations also led me to other historical documents. Thank you to these authors. I consulted Deborah Beck's *Hope in Hell: a history of Darlinghurst Gaol and the National Art School*; however, I also created details that differ from that text. Other works that I consulted include Steve Harris's *Solomon's Noose*, Margaret Atwood's *Alias Grace*, Peter Carey's *True History of the Kelly Gang*, Robert Drewe's *Our Sunshine*, Geraldine Brooks's *Caleb's Crossing*, Hannah Kent's *Burial Rites*, Graeme Macrae Burnet's *His Bloody Project*, Angela Bourke's *The Burning of Bridget Cleary* and Sarah Waters's *Affinity*.

I would like to thank the National Art School, formerly Darlinghurst Gaol, for the tour and the glimpse of the (now closed) tunnels. Thank you to the Bayside Council, for allowing me access to the Bayside Libraries Community History Collection and the Louisa Collins file of former Local Studies Librarian Kathryn Cass, which contained documents from Rebecca Pettit, whom I thank as well. Thank you to the archivists, and in particular Gail Davis of the New South Wales State Archives, and to the

Archives for granting me permission to publish items from their collection. Thank you to the librarians at the Mitchell Library at the State Library of New South Wales and the wonderful Trove collection at the National Library of Australia, which provided access to contemporary newspapers and from where all newspaper quotes were sourced. Thank you to Southern Midlands Council for granting me a writing residency in Oatlands.

A special thank you to the Queensland Literary Awards and to the judges for selecting this manuscript as the winner of the Emerging Queensland Writer – Manuscript Award 2017. Thank you to the Queensland Writers Centre for various workshops and for all you do for writers.

Thank you to my editor Julia Stiles for her attentive read and Lisa White for the cover. Thank you to the team at University of Queensland Press, who have all guided me with such care, especially Publishing Director Madonna Duffy, and the endlessly patient Senior Editor Vanessa Pellatt.

Thank you to special friends: Rowena, Nycole, Tania, Sandra, Tanya, Leanne, Angela, Kerry, Leith, Donelle, Belinda, Ginna, Julie, Hailey, Rose; to generous authors who grew my confidence, sometimes without even knowing it, including Gary Crew, Karen Foxlee, Kim Wilkins, Paul Williams, Gabbie Stroud, Aleesah Darlison, Angela Sunde and Robyn Sheahan-Bright.

I am grateful to my mum and dad for always taking me to the library, wherever we were living at the time. Thank you to my extended family, especially my sisters.

Most importantly, thank you to my TeamLee: Lionel, Jessica, Christian, Hannah, Damon, Callum and Thomas. You make my life beautiful.

Notes

1 *The Sydney Morning Herald*, 20 December 1888, p. 5.
2 Louisa Collins File, Bayside Libraries, Community History Collection, barcode 00894400.
3 *Evening News*, 7 November 1888, p. 6.
4 *The Maitland Mercury and Hunter River General Advertiser*, 29 November 1888, p. 5.
5 *The Brisbane Courier*, 6 December 1888, p. 5.
6 *The Sydney Morning Herald*, 6 December 1888, p. 9.
7 *The Sydney Morning Herald*, 8 December 1888, p. 16.
8 *Evening News*, 8 January 1889, p. 3.
9 *The South Australian Advertiser*, 10 December 1888, p. 5.
10 *Evening News*, 8 January 1889, p. 3.
11 New South Wales State Archives: NSW SA: NRS 2130, Register of Letters Received, 1888 Entry 2663 [5/1847].
12 *Evening News*, 8 January 1889, p. 3.
13 Ibid.
14 *The Sydney Morning Herald*, 27 December 1888, p. 3.
15 *The Brisbane Courier*, 25 December 1888, p. 6.
16 *The Sydney Morning Herald*, 20 December 1888, p. 5.
17 *The Sydney Morning Herald*, 21 December 1888, p. 5.
18 *The Sydney Morning Herald*, 29 December 1888, p. 8.
19 *The Arrow*, 25 February 1899, p. 5.

Additional notes: May Andrews testified on several occasions and her testimony was recorded in court documents and also reported in contemporary newspapers. I have drawn on parts of her testimonies including: 'a box, I saw it ... the week before he died. I had seen it in the kitchen it was a little round box, it had a lid – there was nothing on the outside of the box – there were pictures of rats on it – The picture was red, the rats were red, the rats were on their backs'; and 'I said "look what I have found on the shelf" – it was "Rough on Rats" – I could read it'. These are quotes sourced from May's August 1888 statement. In Chapter 1, I followed Overington's method of amalgamating May's statements, and presuming the questions that may have been asked in court. The reference to Michael Collins seeing green lights and stars is from Mrs Ellen Pettit's statement. Chapters 53 and 54 contain material sourced from Louisa Collins's inquest statement. 'Pull, pull' is from *The Arrow*, 25 February 1899, p. 5. The information for the description of Henry Hall was sourced through his convict record. The yellow-eyed dog and sleeping on the table are a homage to Henry Lawson's *The Drover's Wife*. I have used court statements and newspaper articles throughout this novel and many of the witness statements were also published in newspapers. I utilised the Louisa Collins File, Bayside Libraries, Community History Collection, barcode 00894400; various records at the State Archives of New South Wales including Central Criminal Court Papers, July 1888 Regina v Louisa Collins [9/6758]; and many contemporary newspapers including *The Sydney Morning Herald*, *The Brisbane Courier*, *The Arrow* and *Evening News*. 'The Botany Poisoning Case', *The Sydney Morning Herald*, 27 July 1888, page 4; 'The Judge's Summing Up', *Evening News*, 10 December 1888, page 6; and 'The Botany Murder Case', *Evening News*, 8 January 1889, pages 3 and 4, were particularly useful.